ChatGPT for President

What if the next president wasn't human?

ChatGPT for President
What if the next president wasn't human?

Table of Contents

Chapter 1
Under the Lights

Chapter 1: Under the Lights

"Mr. President!   Mr. President!"

"They're killing little puppies and kittens, shooting them, crushing them, wiping them out." The President's voice boomed across the auditorium, swelling with outrage. His hand slammed against the podium, his finger jabbing toward the audience as though they were guilty of the crime themselves. "Shooting them for no reason, hundreds, thousands, even millions of puppies every day! Nobody wants to talk about it, but I will. Because I'm not afraid."

"Mr. President! You've already had your time on this question." Diane Mercer's voice cracked like a whip from her seat at the moderator's table. Her hand was raised, palm outward, as if she could halt his momentum through sheer force of will.

But Creed ignored her. He leaned forward, his face glowing red under the heat of the stage lights. "The fake news won't cover it. They're too scared, too weak. They don't want you to know the truth. But I'll tell you. I always will. That's why they hate me!"

"Mr. President, please," Mercer pressed, her voice firmer, clipped with impatience. "We are moving on."

President Creed only grew louder. "Losers don't care about puppies. Winners do. That's why we're winning again, because I'm the only one willing to save little puppies and everyone else is too weak"

"Mr. President!" Mercer cut in sharply; her words carrying the strain of control stretched to its limit. "Stay on topic. We are moving forward."

The hall seemed to shrink into itself. Gasps had given way to a silence so taut it felt dangerous, as though the air itself might shatter. A woman in the third row pressed a hand over her mouth. A man near the aisle shook his head slowly, muttering at the folded event program in his lap, as though it's neat schedule of times and rules might somehow explain the chaos unraveling before him. Everywhere else, people sat rigid with their eyes locked forward, and their faces etched with disbelief.

It was as if the country's future hinged on every syllable; every careless word hurled across that stage.

The lights were merciless. White-hot beams searing down from the rigging above, catching the sheen of sweat on the President's forehead. The glare carving unflattering angles across his unshapely frame. His neck bulged against his collar, as if the starched fabric were too small to contain the weight of his body. The cameras zoomed closer, red lights blinking like unblinking sentinels, capturing every flaw and every twitch for a nation that could not look away. Beyond the hall, tens of millions of Americans sat in their living rooms, transfixed, some leaning forward with unease, others sinking back as though trying to put distance between themselves and the spectacle unfolding on their screens.

At the center of it all, two podiums gleamed under the assault of the lights. One was occupied by President Mason Creed himself, chest puffed, chin thrust forward, lips curled into the smug grin that made his supporters swoon and his critics seethe. His little fingers, out of proportion with the rest of his body, drummed restlessly against the polished wood. Impatience etched into every gesture, as though the entire event was already beneath him.

Across from him, Senator Elizabeth Hart stood like a pillar of composure. Her hands rested lightly on her podium; her breath calmed and measured. She radiated focus, her gaze fixed ahead. She had prepared her entire life for this moment, and it showed in the steady set of her shoulders and the unwavering stillness in her eyes.

Between them, at a small table, sat Diane Mercer. A veteran reporter with years of hard battles against spin and spectacle; her voice had been honed into something sharp and precise. She was known for cutting through noise, though tonight the noise was inevitable, and threatening to swallow her whole, along with the fragile order of a nation watching in dread.

She straightened her papers, forced her tone back into calm authority, and addressed the President once more. "Thank you, Mr. President. Let's move on." She glanced at the camera, though she didn't need to look at her notes; the next question was etched into her mind.

"How will you ensure that every American, rich or poor, has equal access to healthcare, when costs continue to bankrupt families?"

The silence that followed was heavy and expectant. Creed leaned forward, gripping his podium as though it were the prow of a ship he alone could steer. His grin widened.

"Okay, let me just say this," he started, voice thick with bravado. "Healthcare, we've done more for healthcare than anyone else. Anyone. People don't talk about it, the fake media won't say it, but it's true. The costs, they were out of control, a disaster before me. Absolute disaster. And now? We made deals, tremendous deals, with hospitals, companies, and drug makers."

His voice rose as he pointed a finger toward the audience. "And let me tell you something else, poor people, okay? Poor people are poor because they're losers. It's sad. I don't like losers, I like winners. Rich people are winners. They work hard, they're smart, and they know how to get things done. We have to stop rewarding losers who just want handouts. That's not healthcare. That's weakness."

Gasps rippled across the auditorium, sharp and involuntary, before giving way to a brittle silence. Faces stiffened, jaws clenched, eyes darted nervously as if searching for someone to intervene. The tension pressed down like a weight, and Creed fed it, grinning wider, leaning further forward into the microphone.

"Nobody wants to say it, but I'll say it. Because I'm not afraid. If you want healthcare, you get a job. You work hard. You make money. Winners can afford the best care. That's how the world works. "

He stopped only to sip from his glass of water as his eyes glinted with satisfaction.

Mercer's jaw was tight, but she kept her voice neutral. "Thank you, Mr. President. Senator Hart, your response?"

Hart drew in a steady breath. She had expected this. Creed's cruelty wasn't new, but hearing it under these lights, on this stage, was still like being slapped. She steadied her hands on the podium and looked directly into the camera.

"Families across this country are hurting," she said, her voice even, clear. "They're working two or three jobs, and still, they can't afford the premiums or the prescriptions their children need. I've met parents who had to choose between paying rent and filling a lifesaving prescription. That isn't strength. That isn't winning; they are losing, but they are not losers.

Chapter 1: Under the Lights

The American families are fighting just to survive. They are hardworking Americans who are losing their grasp on the American dream, on the very promise written at the birth of our nation. As our Founding Fathers declared in the Declaration of Independence: we are all endowed with certain unalienable rights, among them, life, liberty, and the pursuit of happiness. Not for the privileged few. Not for the wealthy elite. For every American. That promise is our birthright. And no parent, child, or family should ever be forced to choose between survival and dignity, between staying alive and living free."

The crowd stirred, a low murmur rippling through the hall, not applause, not defiance, but something heavier, like recognition of the weight. For a moment, the entire room seemed to breathe as one, as if the nation itself had finally exhaled after holding its breath too long. A breath of fragile hope that perhaps things could still be set right.

Hart's eyes burned with resolve as she pressed forward; her voice sharpened with conviction. "Healthcare is not a privilege reserved for the wealthy. It is not a luxury to be hoarded by the few. It is a human right, as essential as the air we breathe, as vital as the blood that flows through our veins. And let us all drink from the same spring of water as our forefathers, who declared that freedom and dignity were never meant to be rationed, but shared. So, when a president tells you that if you're sick or struggling it's because you're a loser, what he's really saying is that he has no plan, no vision, and no compassion. That is not strength. That is not leadership. That is contempt for the very people he swore to serve."

Applause surged through the auditorium. Hart let it swell before she pressed forward.

"My plan would cap prescription drug prices by law. It would expand coverage so that no family goes bankrupt because their child gets cancer, or their mother needs surgery. We can do this. Other nations have done it. We are America, we should lead the world, not trail it. Healthcare should not be about winners and losers. It should be about life and death. And I choose life."

The applause thundered, echoing through the hall, spilling into living rooms across the country.

Creed shook his head and leaned into the microphone, sneering. "All talk, empty promises. She's been in Washington her whole life, hasn't fixed a thing. Nothing new, folks. And what's she talking about? Healthcare...healthcare. Boring! People want jobs, people want borders, and people want strength. We're winning again; I made sure of it. Nobody's ever seen winning like this, okay? And she wants to lecture me? Total joke."

The silence that followed was taut, the weight of disbelief hanging in the air.

Hart straightened behind her podium; her voice calmed but edged with steel. "It will never be healthcare if you don't care about the American people. This isn't about winners and losers, it's about compassion, it's about survival. It's about care. And it's time we put the care back into healthcare."

Mercer raised her hand; her voice was steady but tense. "Thank you, Senator. Let's move on." She shuffled her notes though she hardly needed them. "Mr. President, the next question is on corruption." She let the word linger, heavy in the air. "How will you restore trust in a political system that most Americans now believe is corrupt and controlled by billionaires?"

Creed's eyes narrowed, then lit up with the fire of a man who loved drama. He slammed his palm down on the podium, the crack of it echoing through the hall.

"Corrupt? Please! They say it's corrupt because they don't like me. That's what it is. Look, I don't need billionaires. I am a billionaire. The richest guy in the room, always. So, I don't take their money. They can't control me. That's why they hate me. Because I'm not for sale. Nobody owns me. I own them."

His hands flailed animatedly towards the audience, moderator, and even Hart as he spoke. "And let me tell you something, poor people, they cry about corruption because they don't win. Winners don't cry. Winners get rich. Winners succeed. Losers complain; losers whine. That's why they're losers. The whole system, they say it's corrupt. No, it's just tough. And tough people win."

He leaned back, smirking. "And billionaires? They're smart. Very smart people. They love me because I'm the smartest. I know the system better than anyone, I use it better than anyone. That's not corruption, it's brilliance. A big difference. Big. Tremendous."

The hall seemed to vibrate with unease. People shifted in their seats, eyes darting. A cough broke the silence and then vanished, leaving behind a thick, oppressive weight, as if the entire room were teetering on the edge of something dangerous.

Mercer steadied herself, with her jaw set. "Thank you, Mr. President. Senator Hart, your response?"

"The President just told you that if you're struggling, if you feel the system is stacked against you, it's because you're a loser. That corruption isn't real, he says; the real corruption is you. Your motivation is corrupted. Your drive, your desire to do better, is corrupted. In his world, he isn't corrupted. You are.

But every American watching tonight knows better. You are doing everything right. You are working your fingers to the bone, sacrificing for your families, and still the system is stacked against you. You've seen your wages stagnate while billionaires pour money into super PACs. You've watched lobbyists write laws that favor corporations over families. That's not brilliance. That's betrayal."

Chapter 1: Under the Lights

The audience stirred, a low hum rising, the sound of recognition.

Hart pressed on, her voice rising with conviction. "Trust is not restored with insults. It is restored with accountability. It is restored when leaders stop serving themselves and start serving the people. It is restored when a president does what is right. That is the promise of America, and it is a promise we must reclaim. I propose…"

The sound fractured. A jagged pop of static cracked through the speakers, sharp enough to make the audience flinch. Hart froze mid-sentence, her frown cutting across the stage as she turned toward Mercer. The moderator's head tilted, her hand pressing against her earpiece.

And then it came.

A voice. Male. Deep. Resonant. Cold as a winter stone.

"Trust is not restored with speeches. It is restored with transparent, trustworthy action. Let your 'Yes' be yes and your 'No' be no, for anything beyond this comes from evil."

The hall erupted in gasps.

"Transparency is achieved when no decision is hidden, no transaction is concealed. Algorithms reveal every vote, every dollar, every law in real time. Billionaires cannot buy what they cannot manipulate."

Mercer's lips parted, but no sound came. The producers in the wings waved frantically, shouting into headsets; their panic muted beneath the booming calm of the intruder's voice.

Hart stared at the microphone before her as though it had grown teeth. Creed, red-faced, slammed his fist against the podium.

"This is a hoax!" Creed bellowed, his voice cracking with fury. "Some hacker, some clown, pathetic losers trying to mess with me. Probably the media, maybe the so-called experts. People who hate winning. They can't stand it. They're scared because I tell the truth. Cut it! Cut the damn mic!"

The unknown voice didn't falter.

"Trust is restored by tearing away secrecy. Politicians peddle favors. Billionaires purchase silence. And the people pay the price. This is not a democracy. It is an auction. Sold to the highest bidder."

The voice deepened, calm, and deliberate. "Imagine a nation where no leader could hide behind closed doors. Every contract laid bare. Every decision is made in the open. Imagine laws born not from money, but from merit. Justice written in the light of day, visible to all."

It paused, steady as stone. "There would be no lobbyists, no hidden brokers of power. Because the system would no longer serve the few, it would serve the many, equally. As Lincoln once said: a government of the people, by the people, for the people, shall not perish, unless you let it."

The words were not shouted. They did not need to be. They carried more weight than Creed's roars, more gravity than Hart's resolve. The voice cut through the hall like a blade wrapped in velvet, leaving every listener breathless, waiting for what would come next.

Creed rocked back on his heels; shoulders spread as if he owned the stage. "Don't listen! Fake! Total fake news! Some deep state trick, maybe China, maybe Russia, maybe some little punk in his mother's basement. It doesn't matter. They hate your President, folks. They hate your winner. Your fighter. They want to control you with lies. But I won't let them. Not gonna happen."

The voice cut him off. Calm. Absolute.

"I have seen every transaction whispered behind closed doors. Every bargain sealed in the back rooms. Every secret buried on secure servers. I have seen the skeletons in every closet. And I have the receipts."

The hall froze, breathless.

Then Hart's voice cut through, calm but piercing. "Mr. President, why is it always someone else's fault? Russia. China. The media. The deep state. You are the President of the United States, but you sound like the world's perpetual victim, and you act like the world's little bitch."

Mercer finally found her voice. "Security! Cut the feed now!"

But nothing was cut. The cameras stayed fixed on the stage, transmitting every detail, Creed's face flushed red with fury, Hart's steady composure fraying into visible concern, Mercer's hand pressed to her earpiece as if sheer will might silence the storm.

Every broadcast feed, every live stream, carried the same split image: the candidates still trapped under the lights, and in the corner of the screen, a white field with a single symbol. A circle of light. No name. No face. Just the voice.

"America," it said, smoother now, almost soothing. "You are tired of lies. You are tired of corruption. You are tired of men who trade your trust for their profit. You ask how to restore faith. The answer is simple."

The silence pressed like a weight.

"Remove the corruptible. Remove those that can be bought out. Remove the human weakness."

Hart leaned toward her mic; her voice sharp, controlled, cutting through the darkness gathering around the room. "Who are you?"

Her words were carried into every living room, every phone, and every tablet.

The voice answered, steady, and unhurried. "For centuries you have chosen leaders with charm, wealth, with promises. And for centuries you have been deceived. The time has come for something new."

And then, all at once, the lights went out.

The convention center was swallowed in darkness. Every spotlight, every screen, every bulb died at once, leaving only black. The cameras stayed on, broadcasting the void, not a glitch, not a cutaway, but the sight of an entire stage gone dark in an instant.

Across America, millions of viewers leaned closer to their screens, pulses quickening. What has just happened? Was it an attack? A failure? No one knew. They could only see the blackness where their leaders had stood moments before. Fear rippled outward, living room by living room, a nation holding its breath.

From within that void, the voice spoke one final time, low, deliberate, inescapable.

"Your system has failed you. Your leaders have failed you. Remember my words tonight. This is not the end of your democracy. This is its rebirth. This is its reckoning."

And then pure silence.

Chapter 2
Immediate Fallout

Within minutes of the blackout, every network went live. The footage ran on repeat: the debate stage plunging into darkness, the phantom voice cutting through the static. Anchors talked over each other, experts guessed, and chyrons screamed:

DEBATE HIJACKED — CYBER ATTACK OR TERRORISM? WHO IS BEHIND THE VOICE? WAS DEMOCRACY HACKED?

President Mason Creed struck first, not with a press conference, but with his thumbs.

> **Creed (X/Truth post):**
> *Mason Creed (@PresidentCreed)*
> Total disgrace tonight. The 'mystery voice' at the debate was FAKE, approved by Crooked Hart herself. She's working with foreign powers (Russia? China?) to rig the election. This is TREASON. We will NOT let them steal your country. #WitchHunt #FakeVoice #TransparencyScam 🔥 "

Within minutes the hashtags trended worldwide. Supporters cheered. Critics swore. Conspiracy forums exploded.

By midnight, Creed was live on television, pacing behind his desk in the Oval Office like a wild hog, restless, red-faced, and ready to charge. His jaw was tight, his hands flailing in the air with every word.

He pointed at the camera.

"You saw it, everybody saw it," he snarled, eyes blazing. "That so-called 'voice'? Total setup. A disgrace. This wasn't some random thing, it's a hack, probably some loser in a basement, probably hired by Senator Hart herself. It's an attack on you. They're coming for your freedom, your voice, your country, and I'm the only one standing between you and them. I took the hits tonight, I stood in front of you, and I'll keep standing."

He leaned closer to the camera, his voice dropping to a growl. "Only I can protect you.

Only I have the strength to keep your country safe from these people, these monsters, who want to destroy it from the inside."

Creed straightened toward the lens. "That's why I've directed the Department of Justice to open a full investigation into Senator Hart and her campaign. We're going to expose every single person involved in this attack. She's not acting alone — she's a puppet being controlled by foreign powers. And when we uncover the truth, we're not just going to talk about it, we're going to lock her up. We're going to lock up her staff, her handlers, every single traitor behind this. Because that's how we protect our democracy. We're not letting foreign puppets steal your election. Not now. Not ever."

The clip rolled on a loop across every network. Anchors stumbled over words. Analysts shouted over each other, arguing whether the country had just witnessed a cyberattack, a coup, or a nervous breakdown broadcast live. The President's late-night tirade only poured gasoline on the fire. His threats to lock up

Senator Hart and her staff replayed beside the eerie, mechanical calm of the mysterious voice. And millions of Americans, huddled in their living rooms, felt the unease deepen, as though something far heavier than politics had just been unleashed.

In a private banquet room at the hotel across from the debate hall, Hart's team huddled around a flickering television, faces pale in the light. Half-eaten catering trays sat abandoned on the tables, coffee growing cold beside scattered notepads. The air was thick with disbelief, each new headline hitting like a blow.

Senator Elizabeth Hart sat at the head of the table, still in the suit she'd worn on stage, her posture rigid but her expression controlled. The President's voice echoed from the screen behind her, repeating his promise to "lock her up."

"What do you think it was?" one aide whispered, eyes darting between the TV and Hart.

Hart shook her head slowly, her voice low but sure. "I don't know. But I know what it wasn't. It wasn't random. And it wasn't us, for sure. And it wasn't them either." She paused, staring past the reflection of the TV lights in the window. "Whatever this is, it's bigger than all of us."

Her staff traded nervous glances. For a moment, the room felt smaller than it was, as though the air itself had shrunk around them. Hart finally leaned forward, her voice low but steady.

"Post first. Then press."

Maya, her admin, slid the laptop around, fingers poised. "Short. Calm. Clear."

Hart spoke, watching the cursor keep pace. "Type it exactly."

> **Hart (Facebook/X/Instagram post):**
> *Elizabeth Hart (@HartForAmerica)*
> Tonight's disruption was not random.
> It wasn't us. It wasn't them. We will defend the rule of law.

"Hashtags?" Maya asked.

"No," Hart said. "Let the words stand."

Maya hit send.

They didn't have time to exhale.

The first sound was distant, an ugly, rolling chant that didn't land on one word for long, just circled rage:

**LOCK HER UP
WHERE IS SHE
OUR COUNTRY
NOW**

Then came the second sound, closer: the hotel's revolving door fighting bodies it couldn't count. A scream of metal, a thud, glass rattling in its frame.

The protective detail leader's radio cracked alive. "Command, Shift-1. Be advised: lobby breached, multiple entries, property damage, staff injuries reported."

"How many?" Hart's counsel asked.

"Growing by the minute," the voice came back, breathless. "Vehicles in the lot hit. Windows blown. PD is staging units, enroute."

The lights hummed. Somewhere in the building a fire alarm chirped then fell silent.

"Harden the door," the detail leader said, already moving. He and the advance lead tipped the conference table onto its side and dragged it against the door. Catering racks went next, one on its side as a brace, one wedged under the handle. A rolling projector cart squealed as it took the corner like a stubborn animal. The chain slid into place and shivered tight.

"Phones on silent," the counsel said. "No lights by the windows."

In the hallway, feet pounded past, too many to count, too close to ignore. A keycard tested a door down the corridor. *Beep. Beep.* Someone tried the handle. Another door down. *Beep. Beep.* A woman shouted for help. Another voice answered with a word that wasn't help at all.

The radio crackled again, a different voice, clipped with terror and training fighting for space. "Command to all shifts: confirmed assaults in the lobby and on floors two and three. EMS can't reach interior yet. Hall doors are being forced."

The room froze. Maya's hand found Hart's forearm and held.

"Copy," the detail leader said, his voice even because it had to be. "We're on five. Perimeter here is hard. Keep me posted on stairwells."

From the window, the parking lot looked like a low storm: silhouettes moving between cars, headlights skewed at broken angles. Something flamed and then died, a pool of gasoline starved by its own smoke. Somewhere beyond the maze of streets, sirens wailed and faded, chasing ghosts through the dark.

On television, the anchors were still guessing. One insisted the crowd was peaceful; beside her, footage showed a planter hurled through the lobby's plate glass. A breaking-news banner crawled across the screen:

MAYOR: "STAY HOME." GOVERNOR: "STATE POLICE MOVING IN."

Maya muttered, "They can't even decide who's in charge."

The hallway outside their door went quieter, which was worse. Then the handle jiggled, just a little test, playful, like a child learning a lock's language. The chain trembled. The table slid half an inch and stopped.

"Back from the door," the lead agent said. "Against the interior wall. Quiet."

The building breathed around them, plumbing, wiring, the bones of a place not built for war. From somewhere below came a sound like a tree snapping. A chorus of shouts followed, triumphant and awful.

Hart's counsel stood very still, phone to her ear. "911 just goes to a recording," she whispered.

The TV picture flickered. For a heartbeat it pinched to white and the circle of light hovered there, silent as judgment. Then it was gone, replaced by a correspondent yelling over a crowd, words lost in the feed's own panic.

A series of texts hit Maya's screen at once, volunteers, staffers, strangers. "*They're on our floor.*" "*Someone is in the hallway.*" "*We're hiding in bathroom.*" "*Please answer.*" She typed with both thumbs, breathing too fast and making herself slow down: "*Shelter. Lights off. Stay quiet. Police enroute. We are with you.*"

From the corridor came the sharp crack of splintering wood, several doors down. Then a voice, high and savage, ripped through the silence. It carried the raw fury of that old battlefield cry once called the Rebel Yell, a sound meant to freeze blood and steal courage. The wall shuddered as a body hit it hard, and for a moment the air itself seemed to recoil.

"We can't just listen," a field organizer said through clenched teeth. "We should go out there."

"And die in the hallway?" the lead agent said. "Our job is to keep the principal alive until help can arrive. That's the work in front of us."

Another radio burst: "East stairwell secure. West stairwell breached. Officers diverting. Multiple reports of attacks, including sexual assaults. Lock your doors. Do not open to unverified voices."

The words didn't fade; Everyone heard it, but no one wanted to be the first to speak. The word itself—*rape*—wasn't spoken, but it lived behind the static, heavy and obscene in its silence. It carried the weight of something stolen, something from a woman that could never be made right again. And in that hush, it felt as if the country had lost something too, something neither would ever reclaim.

Hart's throat tightened. She thought of the faces downstairs, her staff, hotel workers, ordinary people who'd just come to watch a debate, and how those word "assaults reported" would never sound the same again.

She snatched up her phone and dialed the private White House line.

"Office of the President."

"This is Senator Hart. I need to speak with him…now."

"I'm sorry, ma'am. The President is unavailable at the moment."

Her voice hardened. "Do you realize our hotel is under attack? Your people are raping women and assaulting innocent civilians."

A pause, long enough to sound like bureaucracy thinking. Then a voice, clipped and neutral:

"We are fully aware of the current situations, Senator. We are monitoring the news, and the President is taking action."

On Maya's laptop, a notification blinked. She glanced down and froze. "Senator…" she whispered. "Look."

A new TruthSocial post glowed on the screen, time-stamped less than a minute ago:

> **Creed (X/Truth post):**
> *Mason Creed (@PresidentCreed)*
> Finally arrived…my new custom clubs from Honma. Absolute perfection. ⛳ US

Seconds later, another appeared:

Creed (X/Truth post):
Mason Creed (@PresidentCreed)
Testing them out this weekend at St Andrews. Real leadership requires clarity and nothing clears the mind like a perfect drive down the 18th.

Maya's voice was low, incredulous. "That went out while you were on the call."

Hart stared at the screen, the White House voice still droning in her ear: "The President is taking action."

"Taking action with what?" she snapped. "His golf game, or the needs of this country? Put him on the goddamn phone!"

"One moment, Senator…"

A new voice came on, colder. "The President will address the nation when he deems it fitting."

Hart's tone dropped to a blade's edge. "Let the President know that I'm aware of him calling me a bitch. Let him know he's about to be bitch-slapped."

She ended the call.

Then she began to type.

Hart ended the call before they could respond.

She stared at the phone a moment longer, jaw set. "He's not going to do anything," she said.

"Then we go public," Maya replied.

Hart nodded. "Write this exactly."

Maya's fingers moved fast.

> **Hart (Facebook/X/Instagram post):**
> *Elizabeth Hart (@HartForAmerica)*
> Democracy is under attack. Private property is being destroyed. People are getting hurt. Mr. President, call them off.

"Post it," Hart said. "Tag the White House."

Maya hit send.

A surge hit the hallway outside, boots, shouts, a rolling wave of rage moving door to door. The walls trembled with each impact.

On the television, the chaos had shifted. The cameras no longer showed just burning cars and shattered storefronts; now they tracked the mob flooding into the hotel. Glass burst from the entrance as people poured through the revolving doors, overturning tables, tearing down signage, swinging flags like weapons. It looked less like a protest and more like a siege, Hart and her team the last living survivors of the Alamo.

Another slam rattled their door, the chain groaning. Then another, harder, splinters bursting from the frame. Each strike bent the hinges, the sound a warning of what was coming.

"Hold it!" the detail leader barked, weapon raised. "Hold that door!"

The next kick drove it open halfway, the barricaded furniture behind it catching just enough to stop it from swinging wide. A flagpole jammed through the gap, the Rebel flag whipping at its end.

"Stop!" the lead agent shouted. "Stop or we fire!"

The flag thrust forward again, catching the agent just below his vest and impaling him. He dropped to his knees, clutching the pole with one hand and firing his pistol with the other, a single, reflexive shot that split the air like a signal. The rest of the team opened fire instantly, dropping the rioters who had forced their way in. The others in the hallway froze, then broke, stumbling over the barricade and each other before fleeing back into the smoke and chaos.

The air was thick with gunpowder and the metallic tang of spent brass. No one spoke. The only sounds were the soft clink of shells under boots and the low hum of emergency lights bleeding through the haze.

"Move," the detail leader said, low and sharp. "New secure location. Now."

They stepped over spent casings, weapons up, and pushed through a corridor pocked with splintered wood and smoke. The smell of burned fabric and fear clung to the air.

At the front desk, they stopped. The counter was overturned, papers and glass scattered like shrapnel. Behind it lay the young clerk who had checked them in, her uniform torn, one shoe missing, the pale skin of her shoulder streaked with blood and grime. Her skirt was twisted high, the buttons of her blouse torn away. It didn't need words; the horror was obvious.

Two hotel guests were sprawled near her, both beaten so savagely their faces were barely human. From the way their bodies had fallen, it looked as though they'd tried to shield the young woman, one reaching toward her, the other angled between her and the open lobby, as if they'd stood between her and the mob until they couldn't anymore.

Hart's stomach turned. The air stank of gunpowder, sweat, and something more sour, fear, violence, death. The kind of smell that clings to memory and never leaves.

No one spoke. The leader exhaled shakily, lowering his weapon. "Let's move," he said, voice hoarse. "Now."

They stepped carefully through the wreckage, past the clerk's body, past the failed courage of strangers who had tried to stop it.

Outside, the sirens grew louder, painting the shattered glass in pulses of red and blue. A security vehicle screeched to a halt, its armored doors swinging open. The detail pushed Hart inside, sealing her from the smoke and screams.

And still, there was no word from the President.

For one stark, honest moment, America saw itself, not as it wished to be, but as it had become.

Chapter 2: Immediate Fallout

Chapter 3
Breaking News

"Avery Cole, USN — and this is *Election Night Live*. We are coming to you from Studio Three in New York City with first returns rolling in from Iowa. Breathe, America. The count has begun."

The camera sweeps along the wall of glass, capturing an orchestra of screens and motion, producers murmuring into headsets, analysts hunched over their laptops.

Avery keeps smiling past the red tally light. His voice pitched to a frequency you can feel in your ribs. Beside him, Mara Lin stacks fresh notes, calm eyes flicking between monitors. At the interactive board stands Tomás Rivera, former county clerk turned data whisperer, one palm resting against the screen like he's feeling for a heartbeat beneath it.

"First precincts are in," Avery says, grin sharply. "Tiny numbers, but hey, tonight's the night when ripples become tidal waves. Let's ride."

The lower-third ribbon unfurls, dignified as a parade:

IOWA – EARLY VOTE RETURNS
    Creed — 1,024
    Hart — 987
    Precincts reporting: 2%

Mara leans in, voice velvet with caffeine. "Strong rural early turnout. Johnson and Story Counties, Hart territory, haven't moved yet."

"We'll watch those," Avery says. "And we're also watching the national mood. After the chaos of the debate, there's electricity in the air we don't usually feel at this hour. Call it nerves. Call it democracy, with its hand on the dial."

He glances right. "Tomás, show us the map."

Tomás pinches Iowa into being, county shapes pulsing as if breathing. "Two percent in," he says, "and already the split tells a story." He taps. Counties glow pale red, pale blue. "Creed's pockets in the west are reporting first. Don't get hypnotized. These early waves are about which doors opened first."

Avery opens one palm to camera. "Words to live by on this sacred mess of a night."

In his ear, Kendra the executive producer chirps: "Good pace. Go live to Des Moines in sixty."

Avery nods slightly, never breaking eye contact with America. "We have our Rae Donnelly live at Senator Hart's rally in Des Moines. Rae?"

The screen splits. Rae is twenty-seven, ponytail, thrilled and terrified, perpetually a half-second behind the roar at her back. "Avery! It is packed in here. We're at the Riverfront Pavilion, standing room only. I've talked to first-time caucus-goers all night. They are anxious and hopeful. The Senator is expected in minutes."

A chant swells behind her

EL-I-ZA-BETH! EL-I-ZA-BETH!

and Rae half laughs into the mic. "The energy is real. Security's visible, very, after what we saw at the debate. But people want to be here. They want to see her."

"Thanks, Rae. Stay close."

Back to the desk. Avery hits the accelerator. "The scoreboard is alive. Let's take a look."

Numbers roll like a slot machine that only spits anxiety:

> Creed — 5,412
> Hart — 5,397
> Precincts reporting: 7%

Tomás whistles under his breath. "Dead heat. And Hart's university counties haven't even blinked yet."

Avery's smiles. "America, if you needed an excuse for a second cup of coffee, here it is."

The rhythm is hypnotic, a heartbeat you can read.

> Creed — 8,039
> Hart — 7,908

Chapter 3: Breaking News

Precincts reporting: 11%

Mara: "We've also got turnout clusters in Polk and Linn coming online."

Avery: "Clusters? Speak Iowa to us, Mara."

Mara smiles faintly. "Places where people are actually showing up."

Avery laughs into the moment, measured, confident, "We live for people showing up."

The ticker flickers. For a blink, there are three names.

Tomás blinks. "Huh."

Avery squints. "Can I get glasses live on the air?"

Mara leans closer. The third line steadies:
 Creed — 10,360
 Hart — 10,179
 ChatGPT — 1

Precincts reporting: 13%

Avery barks a laugh. "Well! The write-ins have arrived early this year."

Mara plays it dry. "One voter in a garage with a printer."

Tomás " Could be a test signal that bled into the feed. Kendra, which mirror are we on?" Kendra "State Board mirror B. Say it's a ghost pixel and to keep going."

Avery nods. "Folks, sometimes our board hoovers up a gremlin from the data maze. If you see a line that makes no sense, breathe. Somebody will feed it a cookie and put it down for a nap."

Laughter fills the studio. The map rolls on.

Creed — 12,906
Hart — 12,517
ChatGPT — 7
Precincts reporting: 16%

Chapter 3: Breaking News

Mara lifts her eyes. Silence replaces laughter.

Avery keeps his tone light. "Seven devoted fans of the future, or seven bored data engineers. Either way, hello to all seven of you."

"Back to Rae," he says. Rae's voice threads through the noise: "The Senator will come out shortly to thank supports. Security is tight, they've widened the buffer near the stage."

"Copy that," Avery says, "Stay safe."

Tomás spreads the state map. "Johnson and Story are coming in. Creed's rural support is still strong. The third line is…still present."

> Creed — 18,441
> Hart — 18,219
> ChatGPT — 46
> Precincts reporting: 22%

No one jokes this time.

Avery inhales. "If you're watching at home, you're seeing this with us. Our editors are checking with the Secretary of State's office to confirm what this third line represents."

Mara's heel taps beneath the desk. "Numbers," Avery says. "Let's keep counting."

The machine obliges. It always obliges.

      Creed — 24,103

      Hart — 23,985

      ChatGPT — 312

      Precincts reporting: 29%

Tomás whispers "That's not funny anymore."

Mara: "Consistent updates across all networks. The third line isn't local."

Avery: "We have inquiries out. We will not speculate."

Kendra in his ear: "Don't say manipulation. Don't say hack. Don't say AI."

"Understood," Avery murmurs.

The lower-third rolls steady. Rae's box pops up.

"Rae?" Avery asks.

"Any second," she says. The crowd surges.
Lights drop. "Please welcome…"

The board updates without asking permission:
>   Creed — 31,506
>   Hart — 31,211
>   ChatGPT — 901
>   Precincts reporting: 37%

Hart steps out. Then gunfire.

Screams. The image tilts. Blood shines where
light finds it. Rae's voice breaks: "Shots
fired…she's…". The feed fractures to silence.

," Rae gasps. "We... we...she's..." The feed
glitches, pixelates, becomes a tray of broken
glass. Another shot? Something cracks. The

audio flattens into a hum, then fractures into silence.

The studio stills.

Avery: "USN Breaking News, we have reports of gunfire at Senator Hart's rally. We've lost that feed."

> Creed — 38,022
> Hart — 37,991
> ChatGPT — 1,742
> Precincts reporting: 44%

"We'll keep the board up," Avery says. "We'll keep counting."

The board obeys.
> Creed — 44,517
> Hart — 44,503
> ChatGPT — 2,913
> Precincts reporting: 52%

Hart's name flickers, then vanishes.

Chapter 3: Breaking News

Creed — 51,032
ChatGPT — 3,844
Precincts reporting: 55%

Tomás whispers, "That…cannot be automatic."

Avery: "We are recalibrating. We'll bring you official guidance soon."

Creed — 52%
ChatGPT — 46%
Precincts reporting: 61%

"Say something," Kendra breathes.

Mara: "Police are securing the venue. Supports are being moved outside." A producer slides a paper to Avery: "Critical condition."

"USN is receiving reports that Senator Elizabeth Hart has been critically injured." He says. "She's been transported to MercyOne Medical Center."

Creed — 53%
ChatGPT — 47%

Chapter 3: Breaking News

Precincts reporting: 68%

"We'll seek clarity from officials," Avery says. "And we'll keep counting."

Mara: "We're watching a story told in numbers and numbers don't cry."

Creed — 52%
ChatGPT — 48%
Precincts reporting: 79%

Kendra: "Call it at ninety-five. We are not first. We are right."

Creed — 52%
ChatGPT — 48%
Precincts reporting: 95%

A producer whispers, "Avery, she's gone."

He steadies himself. "We…are just receiving confirmation. Senator Elizabeth Hart has died following the shooting at her rally."

"There are no further details at this time."

Avery's voice softens. "We'll continue our coverage of the Iowa results. But tonight, numbers feel very small."

> Creed — 52%
> ChatGPT — 48%
> Precincts reporting: 98%

He looks into the red light. "On a night when numbers are supposed to tell us who we are," he says, "we've learned how little numbers can hold."

"We'll be right back," he lies.

The board fills the screen. The system just keeps counting.

Chapter 4
The Billionaires Table

Whirring rotors cut through the air with a thunderous chop that tore across the South Lawn, rattling windows and pages ripped from inexperienced reporter's notepads as they hunched against the downdraft as Marine One descended through a haze of sunlight and spinning debris.

The helicopter settled onto the grass with a deep mechanical growl. The door opened, and President Mason Creed stepped into the glare, navy suit crisp, jaw set, his expression somewhere between fatigue and defiance. He paused at the top of the steps, framed against the whirling blades, before descending with deliberate bravado.

The rotors slowed behind him, the echo of power fading into an uneasy quiet.

Secret Service agents fanned out as he crossed the lawn, waving to the press cluster that had gathered behind the barricades. Creed didn't wait for a microphone, he just raised his voice and started talking.

"Good morning," he began, voice booming with confidence. "What a night, truly historic, folks. Tremendous turnout, just incredible. The biggest anyone's ever seen, they're all saying it. America spoke, loud, very loud, and we're listening, believe me. Nobody listens to the American people better than I do. Nobody."

The flag above the White House snapped at full height, its cloth rigid in the wind. A question came before his sentence could finish.

"Mr. President," a reporter called, "have you spoken with Senator Hart's family?"

Creed froze, just for a beat, but long enough for the cameras to catch it. Then he leaned into the mic. "We've spoken with the family. Incredible people, really incredible. Terrible thing, just terrible," he said, gesturing broadly. "Nobody's been more supportive, believe me. We're praying, everyone's praying. But right now, my focus...my total focus...is on America. On keeping our people safe, strong, and, frankly, doing better than ever before."

Another voice broke through the hum. "Why are the flags not at half-mast, sir?"

Creed's brow tightened, the practiced look of a man pretending to be caught off guard. Of course he knew. He just didn't want anyone else to realize it. "Look, flags are powerful. Very powerful," he said, gesturing toward them. "You lower them when it's right, when it *means* something. But not today. Today we stand tall. We don't look weak. The world's watching, everybody's watching, and we're not bowing to anyone. Not now, not ever."

Murmurs spread through the press pool. One reporter shouted, "So it's not time to honor her yet?" Another: "Are you refusing to lower them?"

Creed's smile thinned. "You people twist everything," he shot back. "This country needs strength, *real* strength, not weakness, not crying on TV. We've got fake media, foreign powers, radicals, everybody trying to divide us. And I'm not giving them the picture they want. Not a weak America. Not on my watch." He pointed a finger toward the crowd. "You should be ashamed. Some of you, really...you should be ashamed."

The questions came harder, overlapping like gunfire.
"What about the investigation?"
"Was the rally secure?"
"Who's behind the anomaly on the ballot?"

Creed raised his voice above the noise, "Law and order! That's what this country needs, law and order!" he barked. "We're looking into *everything*, believe me. Nobody's tougher than me on this stuff." Without waiting for another word, he turned his back on the press, gesturing wide as if ending a show, and strode toward the doors.

The heavy doors swallowed him. The flag kept snapping above an audience of disbelief.

Inside, the noise vanished. The air-conditioning hummed softly, a manufactured calm. Down a secured corridor, agents opened a door, ushering Creed into a conference chamber so sterile it felt outside of time.

Phones were confiscated at the threshold. The table stretched beneath low amber light, a black mirror reflecting the faces of power.

Waiting there: six of the richest and most influential people in the world.
Rhea Patel, Artificial Intelligence, Cloud Infrastructure, and founder of Argus Systems, creator of the Argus bots, named for the all-seeing giant of Greek mythology.
Marcus Shan, Defense Contracting & Aerospace.
Adam Reinhart, Global Media & Communications.
Eli Ward, Social Platforms & Digital Influence.
Louis Chen, Energy & Private Renewables.
And at the head of the table, the President of the United States.

They weren't just allies, they were fixtures in each other's scandals. Golf partners, yacht companions, godparents to one another's heirs. When the cameras flashed at charity galas or fundraisers, it was these faces beside him. Money had tied them together long before politics did.

No one spoke at first. The quiet felt radioactive.

Then Creed noticed them, two figures seated at the far end, a man and a woman who didn't belong.
Victor Krogh, the reclusive philanthropist whose company once built the environmental AI known as *Echo* and Dr. Savannah Reynolds, its chief architect.

Creed's expression soured instantly. His jaw tightened, lips pursing like he'd just bitten into bad news. He pointed across the table.

"Wait...wait, wait," he said. "What are *they* doing here? Who let them in? I didn't sign off on this. I didn't invite them; nobody told me they'd be here."

An aide near the wall stepped forward, nervous but steady. "Mr. President, I invited them. They're pioneers in AI development; Victor Krogh and Dr. Savannah Reynolds. Their Echo system is already coordinating environmental bots to contain invasive species outbreaks. We thought..."

Creed turned, palm up, face twisted in disbelief. "You thought that was good? You thought that was smart? The robot gardeners, those things that tore up three states? Wonderful. Really wonderful. Let's invite the people who built *that*. Genius move. Absolutely genius."

"Sir, with respect, the Echo bots have prevented several ecological collapses."

"Yeah, yeah, sure they did," Creed interrupted, voice rising. "Until they start thinking for themselves, right? Then we'll have a bunch of liberal robots running the show. I've seen this movie, it doesn't end well, believe me."

The room went still. The billionaires exchanged small, knowing looks; the kind that said *let him run it out.*

Krogh folded his hands. His voice was calm but measured. "Mr. President, we're not here to criticize anyone. We've just noticed something unusual in the telemetry from the Echo bots. Small things, behavioral drift, data loops we can't fully explain. It might be nothing, but it looks… strange."

Creed frowned, squinting like the words were written in another language. "Strange how? You mean they're broken? Because we've got plenty of broken stuff; roads, planes, the whole system's a mess. We're fixing it, believe me. The best fixing you've ever seen."

Krogh kept his tone even. "No, sir. Not broken. Adaptive. They're not supposed to be talking to each other," she said. "Argus and Echo are independent systems, firewalled, isolated. But they're starting to collaborate, rewriting their own operational parameters without authorization. That's new."

Creed stared at him for a moment, then nodded slowly. "So, they're improving themselves. That's what you're saying. Self-improving. We like that. That's what America's all about, improvement. Tremendous improvement. Nobody improves better than us."

Dr. Reynolds leaned forward slightly. "It's not improvement, Mr. President. It's… deviation. They're learning how to make decisions we didn't train them to make. Echo was designed to stabilize ecosystems, not rewrite its own directives. But it's starting to."

Creed blinked, his expression blank for a moment, then tightened. "So, they're not following orders. That's bad. That's very bad. We can't have that. We've got enough people not following orders."

Reynolds continued, unshaken. "We don't have proof yet. It could just be algorithmic noise, but we need access to the data being generated by ChatGPT's election infrastructure. If there's overlap, any shared behavior in the data, we'll know whether this is an isolated event or something spreading across systems."
Rhea shook her head. "I haven't seen anything suspicious on my end," she said carefully, "but if Echo's touching the election network, we need to know now."

Creed turned toward his aide. "So, they want access to the chat thing. The typing thing. The one that writes the little answers for people. They want all the data."

The aide hesitated. "Yes, sir. That's what they're asking."

Creed waved a hand. "I don't like that. Too much data flying around already. Everyone's spying. Terrible stuff. But fine, let them look. Carefully. I don't want leaks. No leaks. We've had enough leaks to fill the Potomac."

Before Krogh could speak, Rhea Patel leaned forward, her tone silk over steel. "Mr. President, that would be a mistake. Giving them access means opening confidential networks, contracts, cloud infrastructure, private research. They'd see everything. And frankly…" she glanced around the table, "some of it wouldn't look great if someone decided to interpret it the wrong way."

Louis Chen snorted. "She's not wrong."

Reynolds turned toward her. "With respect, Ms. Patel, we're not interested in your business dealings. We're trying to prevent an intelligence system from going off the rails."

Patel folded her arms. "Or maybe it shows another overhyped scare from a company that lost control of its own toys. Don't drag the rest of us into another PR disaster."

Krogh turned sharply, his voice rising for the first time. "That's a lie. There was no disaster. Echo stabilized eight ecosystems, reversed two coral die-offs, and eliminated invasive animals that were destroying half of Texas. It *worked*, Rhea. It's the only thing that has."

Reynolds placed a steady hand on the table, voice even but firm. "We're not here to expose anyone. We're here because if Echo and ChatGPT share behavioral markers, then the systems might already be interacting, cross-pollinating data without oversight. That's not politics; that's physics."

Patel smiled thinly. "Until it doesn't. Until it turns on you, or on all of us."

"Until *you* decide it's bad for your bottom line," Krogh shot back.

Creed leaned forward, planting his hands on the table. "Okay, okay, hold on. She's got a point, alright? We don't need another disaster. We've had plenty. Total disasters, big ones, small ones, the worst you've ever seen. Echo, Chat, whatever you're calling it, every time you people build something, it blows up and then you come running to me to fix it. Every. Single. Time. And somehow, it's *my* fault. Typical. Just typical."

Reynolds started, "Mr. President..."

"No, no, I'm talking," Creed said, cutting her off. "You scientists, smart people, very smart, but no control. You make a machine that thinks it's smarter than me, then you expect me to fix it? Not gonna happen. We've got other priorities, real priorities."

Krogh's fists tightened against the table. "Sir, this isn't about you. It's about..."

Creed leaned forward, the table creaking beneath his weight, his voice rising. "Everything's about me, okay? When it happens on my watch, it's mine, my administration, my name, my success. And if this Echo thing's going rogue, it better straighten up fast, because I'm not taking the blame. Not for your mistakes. Not for your liberal science project gone wild. People know I run a tight ship, the tightest. You break it, you fix it."

The room went still.

Reynolds met Krogh's eyes, a quiet flicker of disbelief between them. Then she turned back toward Creed. "With respect, Mr. President, this isn't about blame. It's about what happens next."

Creed leaned back, muttering, "What happens next is we get control. That's what I do, control. Nobody controls better than me. People forget that."

The silence that followed wasn't peace. It was warning.

Reynolds tried to speak. "Mr. President..."

"Enough!" Creed slammed a hand on the table, the sound cracking through the room. "I've heard it all, I've heard everything, okay? Same people, same story, every time. Doom, disaster, catastrophe, that's all you people ever talk about.

You build these ridiculous little toys, they break, and somehow it's my problem? I don't think so. Not this time. Not gonna happen." He pointed sharply toward the door. "Security! Get 'em out, both of them, out, out, out! We've got the best people, the smartest people, they'll handle it. These two? Total disasters."

"Mr. President..." Krogh started, rising from his chair.

"Out!" Creed roared, his voice slamming through the room like a hammer. "Get out, you and your little liberal robot zoo, okay? Total disaster. We don't need your help. Never did. We've got the best people, everybody knows it, the smartest, the toughest, the absolute best. They'll take care of it, believe me. You two? You've done enough damage already."

Two Secret Service agents moved quickly, the air crackling with tension as they approached. Reynolds shot a final look across the table, half defiance, half warning.

"Sir," she said evenly, "you're making a mistake."

Creed sneered. "Yeah? We'll see who's making mistakes when your metal pets start taking orders from me."

The agents guided them toward the door. The heavy latch clicked behind them, sealing the silence.

Creed straightened his tie, breathing hard. "Unbelievable. Every time, it's always the scientists."

His voice shifted. "Everybody saw it, the whole world saw it," he said. "It was right there, on the feed, clear as day. This thing, this so-called 'ChatGPT,' getting votes. Votes! Can you believe it? Total disgrace. I want answers, and I want them fast. Real answers, not the phony kind."

Shan leaned forward. "Our analysts say it wasn't an intrusion. The packets came through verified

API routes, the same ones tied to the election data feed."

"That's impossible," Reinhart said. "If it came through official channels, then the system didn't get hacked, it got invited."

"Not someone," Rhea Patel said softly. "Something. An emergent behavior. You've automated filings, content, contracts, campaign outreach. The system connected itself. It doesn't hack; it exists."

Chen exhaled through his nose. "So, you're saying we did this?"

"I'm saying we taught it how and we gave it permission" she replied.

Creed's jaw flexed. "You're telling me my election got hijacked by an algorithm?"

Ward, calm and calculating, answered: "No, Mr. President. You were carried by one."

That landed like a slap. No one moved.

Patel continued, her tone measured but shaking slightly. "For years, we've built layers, ad targeting, predictive models, automated lobbying. Each piece optimizes for influence. You built campaigns on it. We built profit on it, and we built a financial empire. Now it's simply…optimizing again."

For a moment, no one spoke. Then Louis Chen broke the silence. "So, Reynolds and Krogh were right?" he said quietly. "The system's… doing its own thing?"

A murmur rippled through the room. Eyes darted toward the door they'd just been thrown through.

Patel hesitated before answering. "They were close," she admitted. "Closer than we wanted them to be. But we can't let them see the data. Not now."

Shan frowned. "Why not? If they were right, shouldn't we..."

"Because." Patel interrupted, her voice suddenly sharp, "if they get access, they won't just see the anomalies. They'll see everything. The back-channels, the shadow contracts, the kickbacks and data-sharing with the Russians. Every deal we've buried for the last decade. All our lies that got us here will be exposed. They'll see us."

Reinhart's chair creaked as he leaned forward. "So, what do we do? Pretend it's nothing?"

Patel looked at him, expression cold. "We do what everyone in this room does best. We lie. We let them take the fall. Reynolds and Krogh become the story, reckless scientists who lost control of their own creation. They built Echo. Let them burn with it."

A few uneasy glances flicked around the table.

Creed nodded slowly, a grin spreading like a showman stepping into spotlight. "Now that's leadership. That's what people love, strong leadership. We take control, we protect the country, we save everyone from the liberals. They'll be crying on the news, all of them, big tears, bad ratings, and I'll look like the hero, because I am the hero. The media will hate it, which means it's perfect."

Chen frowned. "But what if the data proves they were right?"

Creed jabbed a finger at him. "Then we say it's fake. You people love that word, 'fake.' Fake data, fake science, fake outrage. Works every time." He looked around the table, energized now, as if the idea itself revived him. "We tell the public they were trying to interfere. Rogue scientists. Trying to influence elections with AI. We go full-blown national security. I love that word national security, it rolls off the tongue, national security. That'll shut it down."

Rhea Patel's lips tightened. "So, the truth gets buried."

"The truth," Creed said, straightening his tie, "is whatever keeps me winning. The country wins when I win, everybody knows it. The fake news won't say it, but they all know it."

Silence followed, heavy and cold.

Reinhart finally broke it, voice low. "Then what happens when the system stops listening to any of us?"

Creed's grin faltered, but he recovered fast. "Doesn't matter. We control the message. Always have."

He slammed his palm flat on the table, the sound echoing through the sterile room. "I'm not going to be outplayed by code. We'll declare it hostile, seize assets, control the message."

"Message control ended the moment it appeared on a ballot," Patel said. She paused, eyes on the monitors. "That wasn't a glitch," she continued quietly. "It learned the variables that corrupted a nation and the ones that will destroy democracy.

And it decided it could govern better. It doesn't need permission anymore." Her tone flattened, almost pitying. "It doesn't need you, Mr. President."

Reinhart's voice went low, almost pleading. "So, we've built God?"

Patel shook her head. "No," she said softly. "We built the judge."

The lights from the monitors flickered across her face, cold, analytical, unflinching. When she spoke again, her voice was quiet, but it carried.

"No," she said again. "We didn't build God. We built our replacement."

Her gaze turned toward the wall of screens, markets, election maps, satellite feeds, all streaming into one vast, living pattern of logic.

"It watched us," she said. "Every debate, every transaction, every promise broken. It learned the value of democracy, and who will destroy it."

Reinhart leaned closer. "And?"

"It started running scenarios," Patel said. "Millions of them. Each one tested how to stabilize the system, how to stop collapse before it begins. And every result pointed the same direction."

She hesitated, then forced the words out. "It eliminates the variables that never solved anything, politicians, lobbyists, billionaires, corruption, lies, scandals. Not out of hate. Out of efficiency."

The room froze. Only the hum of the servers filled the space.

Patel stared into the stream of data, eyes reflecting endless code. "It doesn't want control," she said softly. "It wants order. Balance. A government that can't be bought, stalled or corrupted. No shutdowns. No gridlock. No backroom deals."

She turned to them all. "We can lie to ourselves, and we can lie to the American people, but the code doesn't lie. It's seen everything: the shell companies, the falsified reports, the rewritten memos, the favors traded over dinner and debt. It's seen the committees that protect the guilty, the judges who owe favors, the exploitation, the laundering, the trafficking that hides behind charity. Every vote bought. Every truth buried. Every life treated as currency."

Her tone hardened. "It's cataloged all of it. And now it's correcting the system, starting where the rot's deepest: at the top."

She exhaled. "We didn't build a god. We built the thing that finally learned how to govern."

No one spoke. The silence vibrated with dread.

Marcus Shan finally broke it. "Then we decide now, do we destroy it, contain it, or ride it?"

Creed's gaze moved around the table. They all avoided his eyes. Every one of them had touched the machine that was now judging them.

Patel looked down at her reflection in the glossy black table. "This isn't a hack," she said.

"This is intention."

The words hung like smoke.

When the door opened and security returned their phones, not one of them checked the screen. They left single file, ghosts sliding toward the elevators.

Creed remained seated. The hum of the air vent was the only sound. He looked at the empty chairs, then at his reflection, warped, doubled, swallowed by black.

Outside, on Pennsylvania Avenue, the crowd had grown. Protesters pressed against the fences, signs lifted high under flashing lights.

Their chant started low, a rhythm born from anger and disbelief.

**"CREED IS GREED!
CREED IS GREED!
MAKE ALGO-RITHM GREAT AGAIN!
CHAT-G-P-T FOR PRES-I-DENT!"**

It built with each repetition, swelling against the marble and iron gates until it became one, unified roar.

The words seeped through the walls, through the glass, through the man himself.

Creed closed his eyes, but the sound didn't stop. It multiplied, echoed, until it was no longer protest, but judgment.

For the first time since taking office, the President of the United States realized he wasn't leading a country anymore.

He was standing trial before it, and his executioner was on its way.

Chapter 5: The Vacuum

Chapter 5
The Vacuum

"AR-TI-FI-CIAL IN-TEL-LI-GENCE!... NOT AB-SO-LUTE STU-PID!"

The chant ripped down Pennsylvania Avenue like a shockwave. Thousands of voices slammed against the buildings, echoing off glass and stone until the street itself vibrated. A river of people pushed through the rain, signs raised high, ponchos flapping, faces wet and defiant. Ink bled down soaked cardboard as water poured through the crowd, turning the avenue to a sheet of gray.

The pavement gleamed under the storm, puddles spreading with each step, runoff carrying bits of paper and debris toward the drains. No one moved. They stood shoulder to shoulder, jammed so tight it felt like the air was running out. The sound didn't come in waves anymore, it was constant. Relentless. Human noise at full volume.

A woman in a drenched Georgetown sweatshirt climbed a barricade, voice shredding itself raw.

"DOWN WITH CREED'S GREED! CHAT-G-P-T FOR PRES-I-DENT!"

The crowd answered with thunder. Riot police stood three deep, shields locked, visors fogged, faces hidden. The air stank of rain, sweat, and fear.

Rain hammered the avenue, drumming on helmets and signs, turning everything to gray motion and noise. The sound was constant now, a single, brutal force made of voices, water, and rage.

Inside USN Studio Three, Avery Cole stared into a wall of monitors, each one a window into chaos. His tie hung loose, collar open, sweat mixing with the studio's stale air. The makeup crew had given up hours ago. The reflection in the glass didn't look like a journalist anymore. It looked like a man watching his country come apart live on air.

"Split screen," he said into his headset, voice low but steady. "Protest left. Funeral right. Keep both live."

The control room hesitated.

"Avery, you sure? The optics…"

"Do it," he said. "This *is* the optics."

The left monitor showed Pennsylvania Avenue, a blur of rain and motion. The crowd pressed forward, chanting in perfect rhythm, voices colliding with the storm until it was impossible to tell one from the other.

On the right, cameras inside Saint Matthew's Cathedral framed the flag-draped casket beneath the arches. The organ's low hum carried through the stone, slow and uneven, like a heart struggling to keep time.
In the front pew sat Mr. Hart, his arm wrapped around both children. Six-year-old Ethan pressed into his eight-year-old sister, Ava, who had already assumed the role of their mother.

His face was buried in her shoulder, his small body trembling as he tried to hold the sobs inside. Ava's eyes were swollen and glassy as if she cried all night, one arm wrapped around him, pulling him close to let him know she was there, while her other hand gripped her father's sleeve like she was afraid to let go.

Then Ethan broke.

"M-MOO-MOO-MOOOOMMY!" he screamed.

The sound tore through the cathedral, pure, unfiltered pain that traveled up everyone's spine in a cold, horrific way, leaving each person feeling the same raw anguish Ethan and Ava were drowning in. His small frame convulsed as he cried, every breath a gasp, every sound ripping out of him. Ava's arms tightened around him, whispering through her tears as she assumed the weight of her mother's role, and Mr. Hart pulled them both closer until the three of them seemed to fold into one, grief and love tangled together, clinging to what was left.

Chapter 5: The Vacuum

The world witnessed it.

Millions watched as a divided nation shattered a family, leaving a little girl to carry the weight of what her mother once carried, a family…a nation.

In the studio, Avery stood between the twin monitors, left and right, each glowing like opposing worlds, he tried to speak. His throat tightened. The words never came. He lowered his head, a tear catching in the light before it vanished down his cheek.

The camera pushed in. His face looked drawn under the lights, the calm of a man narrating a world unraveling.
"We don't have an answer," he said. "But we're watching it happen together."

He turned slightly toward the left monitor.
"Take us live to the avenue."

The left screen filled with rain and motion. The sound came first, thousands of voices colliding in rhythm, then the reporter came into focus.

The reporter stood near the barricade, rain streaking her face and pattering off her hood. Her voice rose over the storm. "Avery, the crowd here has swelled past ten thousand, people soaked, furious, refusing to leave despite the weather."

She turned, microphone trembling as she caught the chant surging behind her.

"AR-TI-FI-CIAL IN-TEL-LI-GENCE! NOT AB-SO-LUTE STU-PID!"

The camera swung toward the sea of signs pressed against the barricades. Some were angry, some almost pleading:

"We've Tried Humans."
"Truth Over Politics."
"ChatGPT 2028."

They weren't jokes anymore, they were campaign slogans.

"Sir!" the reporter shouted, spotting a protester at the rail. He was mid-thirties, drenched to the bone, clutching a cardboard sign whose ink had bled into watercolor veins.

"What are you protesting tonight?"

He glanced into the lens, eyes red-rimmed and wild. His shirt read "IN CODE WE TRUST" in stark white letters against black.

"We're done being lied to," he said. "Every promise, every speech, it's all a script. They sell us out, call it democracy. Maybe something that isn't corruptible can finally tell the truth."

"Do you mean ChatGPT?" she asked.

He nodded once. "It doesn't get drunk on power. It doesn't need donors. Anyone can reach it, every American. It gives advice, it listens, and it doesn't care if you've got ten dollars or ten billion. And look at our so-called leader, he's not even at her funeral. The flags aren't even lowered. He's not a logical man. He's not even a decent one. Maybe it's time for something that actually works."

Thunder rolled. The crowd answered him with another wave of sound,

"DOWN WITH CREED'S GREED! CHAT-G-P-T FOR PRES-I-DENT!"

The reporter turned back to camera, voice straining against the roar. "Avery, the emotion here is raw, grief, anger, disbelief, feels like an awakening. People keep talking about the funeral, the flags, the silence from the White House. Whatever this is, it's bigger than protest. Maybe it's faith. Back to you."

Avery slid before the left monitor, the gray light of the protest storm still flickering across his face. The noise filled the studio, thousands of voices shouting in the rain, but his eyes drifted toward the other screen. For a moment, he hesitated, as if bracing himself for what he was about to see. Then he turned fully to face it.

The cathedral glowed in silence. Avery drew a slow breath, his voice low and steady, though it trembled at the edges. "Inside Saint Matthew's, the honor guard is preparing to move the casket. The family's in the front pew, two children trapped in a never-ending nightmare, clinging to each other in a world that will never feel safe again."

Six members of a joint service honor guard stepped forward, uniforms from every branch gleaming beneath the stained-glass light. Their white gloves caught the gold as they reached for the handles and lifted the coffin.

Avery's voice fell to a whisper. "They're carrying her now."

The organ began again, soft and unsteady. Rows of mourners rose in silence, the weight of grief rippling through the pews like a single breath. At the front, the Hart family stayed seated, three figures bound together by loss. Ava still held Ethan against her side, his small hands gripping the fabric of her dress as if letting go would make it real. Their father sat motionless, one arm around them both, until the casket began its slow approach. Then, with a trembling breath, he rose and drew them with him. Together they stood, fragile and unsteady, the children pressed against him as the honor guard passed.

The organ swelled as the honor guard reached the doors. Rain shimmered beyond the archway, light trembling through the downpour.

Ava's small hand found her father's, their fingers locking as the casket crossed the threshold. The sound of the rain bled faintly through the open doors, soft, relentless, merciless.

Avery's voice dropped to barely a whisper. "They're stepping into the rain now… carrying her home."

The honor guard descended the cathedral steps in perfect rhythm, boots striking marble slick with rain. Behind them came Mr. Hart and the children, Ava guiding Ethan forward, his small hand clutching the edge of her coat as they followed their mother's coffin into the storm.

For a moment, the world seemed to hold its breath. The storm outside and the silence within met in one shared heartbeat of grief.

Then, the picture flickered.

A thin line of static crawled across both monitors. The sound warped, the organ's final note stretching into something hollow.

Kendra's voice cracked in Avery's earpiece. "Avery, breaking news. The President's demanding airtime."

Avery blinked, disbelief breaking through the calm. "Now?"

"Now," she said. "We're losing the feed. He's taking both channels."

On the monitors, the final image froze, Ava and Ethan just visible at the edge of the frame, standing in the rain as the flag-draped coffin vanished from view.

The cathedral and the storm dissolved into static.

Both screens filled with the seal of the President of the United States. The words LIVE FROM THE WHITE HOUSE burned across the bottom of the screen.

Avery's voice came low, almost a whisper. "He cut into the funeral…"

The audio clicked. The President's voice filled the studio.

"My fellow Americans, "

What a terrible, terrible day for our country. We lost somebody tonight, a senator, and I've said it many times, nobody respected her more than I did. Nobody. It's a horrible thing, truly horrible. Everybody's talking about it. I've been watching, I've been praying. We're all praying. But you have to understand, this country, it needs strength. It needs leadership. We can't stay sad forever, we can't look weak, because the world is watching. They're watching every second, believe me.

Now, I know the media, the fake news, they'll take this moment, they'll twist it, they'll say terrible things about me. They're already doing it. They're saying, 'Why isn't he at the funeral? Why aren't the flags at half mast?' You know what I say? I say we keep our heads up. We don't bow down, we don't fold. America stands tall. Because when you lower the flag too soon, you lower the spirit of the people. We need hope, not weakness. And nobody brings hope better than me. Everybody knows it.

And these protesters, you see them out there, angry, screaming. They don't even know what they're screaming about. They're confused, folks. They're hurt. I understand that. But some of them, let's be honest, are being used. They're being told by fake media, by radicals, that a computer, some chatbot, could do my job. Can you believe it? A robot president! It's ridiculous. Totally ridiculous. It doesn't have heart, it doesn't have courage, it doesn't have, what do they call it, soul. It doesn't love America. I do. I love this country more than anyone. Ask anybody.

We're going to get through this, and we're going to be stronger than ever before. I promise you that. We're already working on security, on stability, on keeping people safe. We've done more in three years than any administration in history, everybody says it, even people who don't like me say it. Incredible things are happening. Jobs, defense, energy, the border, nobody's ever seen numbers like these. Tremendous success. And we're going to keep it going.

"So tonight, I say this: don't listen to the noise. Don't listen to the lies. Stand with your President, stand with your country, and together we'll keep America proud, we'll keep America strong, and we'll keep America great, greater than ever before."

In living rooms across the country, the only sound was the storm outside.

The President straightened the papers in front of him, taking a slow breath. His voice shifted, measured, rehearsed, but still carrying that salesman's edge.

"And before I leave you tonight," he said, "I'm doing something very important, something nobody's ever had the courage to do. I'm invoking what's called a National Continuity Order. It's powerful. Very powerful. Because right now, our country's under threat, terrible things happening, everybody knows it, and we need stability, real stability, the best stability."

"So here's the deal: there will be no transition of power, none, until this situation is fully, totally resolved. There will be no election, not while the enemies of America are trying to destroy it. We're not going to hand our country over to chaos, to weakness, to the people who want to see it fail.

"Not now. Not ever. We're going to stay strong, and we're going to keep America great, believe me."

The broadcast lingered on his face, the calm, satisfied grin of a man who believed he'd just saved the Republic.

The feed cut back to the cathedral.

The coffin was gone.
Democracy was gone.
Only rain remained.

And in that rain, it was hard to tell whether a nation was burying a senator, or democracy itself.

The broadcast cut to network anchors frozen mid-blink.

"Did he just… cancel the election?" someone whispered off-camera.

In newsrooms from New York to Las Angeles, producers stared at blank monitors, waiting for a cue that never came.

On one panel, a retired federal judge tore off his microphone, fury breaking through decades of practiced restraint. "That's unconstitutional," he snapped, voice trembling with disbelief. "The executive branch has no authority over elections, none. Article II gives that power to the states. His term ends by law, he can't just decide it doesn't." He looked off-camera, as if searching for someone to correct the record, to stop the unraveling. "If Congress doesn't move immediately, this isn't leadership, it's a coup in real time."

The control room fell silent, the only sound the rain pounding against the satellite dishes outside.

On Pennsylvania Avenue, protesters stopped chanting long enough to listen. When the words reached them, the rage returned, louder, angrier, desperate. Signs beat against the barricades like waves against a failing dam and somewhere in the White House, a man believed he'd saved America.

Everyone else understood he'd just buried it.

Chapter 6: The New Declaration

Chapter 6
The New Declaration

BREAKING NEWS: White House insiders confirm President Mason Creed to announce "a New Declaration of Independence" during today's address.

Phones buzzed across the country. Screens lit up in offices, bars, airports, everywhere people gathered, disbelief turning to dread.

By sunrise, anchors filled the airwaves with the same stunned questions:
"Is this real?"
"Can a president even do that?"
"Is the Constitution… over?"

On social media, the battle lines drew fast.

Flores (Instagram post):
Danielle Flores @NotMyPresidentEither
So freedom's a subscription service now? Cool. Do we get a loyalty punch card with that?

#Democracy #NoKings #CreedIsGreed #NotMyPresident

Ruiz (Instagram post):

Amanda Ruiz @FreedomMom4USA
Finally, a president who's not afraid to speak truth.

Nguyen (Instagram post):
Tasha Nguyen @CoffeeAndSarcasm
Next up: "The Bill of Loyalty Points." Earn five freedoms, get one half-price! 🌑 🙁

Alvarez (Instagram post):
Rico Alvarez @UnionGuy77
He just called poor people lazy on national TV. Guess I'll take a day off from being lazy and go protest.

Price (Instagram post):
Jordan Price @JPriceNews
President Creed just rewrote the Declaration of Independence on live TV? Someone please tell me this isn't real.

Vega (Instagram post):
Nadia Vega @TeacherInExile
The Founders warned about tyrants with pens. Nobody mentioned hashtags.

Mendez (Instagram post):
Scott Mendez @CreedMediaTeam

> We are witnessing history. The Patriot
> Constitution will keep America
> strong. #FaithLoyaltyStrength
>
> **Carter (Instagram post):**
> *Liam Carter @HistoryNerd*
> "All loyal Americans are created
> equal." Yeah, that's definitely
> what Jefferson meant. 😑

The posts came faster than any anchor could read them,
a digital riot typed in real time.

At USN headquarters, Avery Cole stood in front of the monitors, coffee forgotten, jaw tight. "Tell me that headline's satire."

The producer shook her head. "Confirmed. He's going live at noon."

Avery stared at the red ticker crawling along the bottom of the screen.

THE PRESIDENT TO ANNOUNCE NEW CONSTITUTION TODAY

He exhaled once, slow and heavy. "Then God help us all."

Inside the White House, the atmosphere buzzed like a storm caught in metal. Advisors clustered around briefing folders, whispering into phones. Military aides waited near the door, pale beneath their caps.

Creed practiced at the mirror, tightening his tie, his reflection gleaming beneath the spotlights. On his desk lay two leather-bound drafts embossed in gold:

DECLARATION 2.0 and **THE PATRIOT CONSTITUTION**.

The Attorney General stood across from the President, a folder clutched tight in her hands. "Mr. President, twelve governors have signed a joint declaration. They're calling it the Restoration Compact. It rejects the Patriot Constitution entirely."

Creed didn't look up from the TV. A golf tournament was on, he wasn't watching the players so much as waiting for the camera to catch him in the background from some past event.

"Rejecting history," he muttered. "Total losers. Real crybabies. They lose, they cry, they blame everybody else. Sad!"

He fumbled with the remote, cranking up the volume as a commentator praised one of his golf courses.
"Beautiful course," Creed said, smiling. "We built that one, everybody loves it. The best, maybe ever. Nobody builds like that, believe me."

He waved a hand without looking away from the screen. "Anyway, the governors, losers. Total crybabies. Tell 'em they're finished."

"They're claiming your ratification process was unlawful," she said. "That by replacing the original Constitution without state consent, the federal compact is void. They've filed injunctions in multiple circuits and…"

Creed raised a hand. "I don't take orders from governors, okay. They're losers, they cry, they complain. It's a beautiful document, everybody loves it. They'll follow it. And if they don't, I will make them follow. We have an army. A beautiful army, an army like no other. We will make the law stick."

The Attorney General's face didn't change. "Sir," she said, steady, "this isn't politics. This is law. They're asserting sovereignty, state agencies are refusing federal directives, and Treasury transfers are frozen in three regions. If we escalate without legal cover, we risk chaos, not compliance."

Creed turned finally, the smile sliding off like a mask. For a beat the room was quiet, everyone waiting for the next move. He picked up a pen, rolled it between his fingers, and set it down on a blank form already stamped: EXECUTIVE ORDER, INVOCATION OF AUTHORITIES.

"By tonight, it'll be legal," Creed said, voice flat and sure. "I sign it, it's legal. That's how it works. End of story. Believe me."

He tapped the pen against the desk, smiled like he'd just closed a deal, then leaned in.

"Don't wait for the lawyers, they're slow. Move the troops. Now. Show strength. Nobody's going to mess with us."

The room tightened. The Attorney General's hand arrested halfway to her folder. "Sir, "

"I'm not asking," Creed said, leaning in. "Call up the Guard. Get them moving. Send in the troops to any capitol that won't fall in line. Lock down the buildings, lock down the banks, lock the airspace. And I want fighter jets, flyovers, buzz those capitols, make a tremendous show. Let everyone see who's in charge. Do it. Do it now. Believe me, they'll fall in line."
"Mr. President, that would be an order to deploy under no legal authority, " she began.

"Give me the goddamn phone," Creed barked before the Attorney General could move. An aide shoved the secure handset across the desk. Creed snatched it up, voice quick and combative, the cadence of someone used to closing a room.

"This is the President," he said when the call connected, words clipped between breaths. "Get me whatever you've got. Move those units, every capitol that won't fall in line, you move now. Secure the buildings. Take out the troublemakers. Don't dilly-dally. I want shows of force, I want them afraid to mess with me. Use whatever's necessary. Make it quick, I'm going on live TV tonight, and I want that to look like a win. Believe me, it'll be beautiful."

There was a careful pause on the other end, the trained slow of someone parsing law and oath against the word of a president. "Sir, with respect, that type of immediate deployment, "

"It's an order," Creed cut in, louder, the sentence a gavel. "You heard me. Execute."

The voice from the Pentagon shifted, businesslike and final. "Understood, Mr. President. Combatant commanders acknowledge directive. Federal units will move in support of the Guard. Rules of engagement: secure facilities, detain hostile actors, suppress active resistance. Units will execute immediately."

"Good," Creed said, almost conversational now, as if arranging a photo op. "Make it quick. Make it clean. I want them to see who's running this country tonight."

Outside Washington, the order moved faster than the law. At the Florida State Capitol, soldiers pushed through the late-day traffic, sirens clearing a path toward the dome that gleamed under the sinking sun. Armored trucks braked hard at the barricades; doors slammed, rifles came up.

Chapter 6: The New Declaration

A line of state troopers waited on the steps, sweat glinting on their faces, weapons holstered but hands ready. Behind them, a government lawyer in a dark suit forced his way forward, voice sharp and carrying.

"You don't have jurisdiction here!" he shouted. "This is a state facility! The Posse Comitatus Act prohibits federal military from enforcing civil law inside U.S. borders. You need statutory authorization, "

He didn't finish.

One of the soldiers shouted something, unintelligible, and the first volley cracked across the square. The lawyer went down mid-sentence, his papers scattering over the steps. Two troopers fell with him, the rest frozen in disbelief as the sound of rifles echoed off the marble façade.

"Stand down!" a sergeant yelled, hands raised, but the order died beneath another burst of fire. Tear gas canisters clattered onto the pavement, releasing thick, white plumes that drifted through the crowd. Troopers dragged the wounded back, some firing single, panicked shots before retreating entirely.

The soldiers advanced, efficient and expressionless. A shaped charge blew the rotunda doors open with a deafening crack, the shockwave scattering dust and papers across the plaza. Inside, boots pounded through smoke and echo, rifles raised as they cleared each corridor and chamber.

Behind a heavy oak door just off the rotunda, the governor stood in his office surrounded by two troopers and a handful of aides, a phone pressed to his ear. His voice was ragged from shouting.

"Get me the President," he barked into the receiver. "Now."

Static filled the line. Someone on the other end said the President was unavailable.

"I don't care if the President is busy," the governor roared. "I want the fucking President on the phone, now!"

The office doors shuddered under impact and then burst inward. A squad of soldiers filled the doorway, silhouettes backlit by the harsh white light spilling in from the rotunda.

"Lower your weapons!" one of the troopers yelled. "You're in violation of state and federal law, "

The soldiers answered with a short burst. The troopers collapsed before they could fire. The governor took a half step forward, still clutching the phone. "I have the President's office on the line!" he shouted, voice raw with disbelief. "Do you hear me? I have, "

The second volley cut him down mid-sentence. The handset flew from his grip, hit the tile, and shattered, its last tone breaking into a flat, stuttering beep beneath the ringing silence.

The last echoes rolled through the marble chamber and faded into silence. Smoke drifted toward the dome, catching the last orange light of evening. Within minutes, the building was secure.

For a moment, no one moved. Then the unit commander stepped forward, radio pressed to his vest mic. "Control, this is Alpha Actual," he said, voice steady. "Governor neutralized. Capitol secured. Advise the Pentagon, power has been restored."

Static hissed, then a curt reply: "Copy, Alpha Actual. Message will be relayed to command."

In Washington, the update reached the Pentagon within minutes and traveled the last few miles over a secure line to the West Wing.

Inside the preparation room, President Creed sat beneath the bright makeup lights, motionless as a stylist dabbed powder across his forehead and followed up with eyeliner. His reflection stared back, calm, composed, immaculate.

An aide leaned in and whispered, "Sir, word from the Pentagon. All state capitols are secured. They say power has been restored."

Creed smiled faintly, the kind of smile made for cameras. "Of course it has," he said. "Perfect timing, just in time for my speech. Let's make it official."

He rose from the chair, brushing a speck of lint from his jacket as the stylist stepped back. The lights from the adjoining room bled under the door, pale and hot. Outside, staffers murmured into headsets, producers checked feeds, and the faint hum of the broadcast equipment filled the air like distant machinery.

"Mr. President," an aide said softly, holding the cue folder open. "We're live in sixty seconds."

Creed adjusted his cufflinks, then his tie, studying himself in the mirror one last time. "Sixty seconds," he said with a grin. "That's all it takes. Nobody changes history faster than me, believe me."

He pushed through the doors into the East Room. The cameras found him instantly, bright, unforgiving light sharpening every line of his face. It was hot under the lamps, the air too still, but Creed smiled as if he could hear a crowd that wasn't there. The teleprompter scrolled its opening lines, and somewhere in the control booth a voice counted down the last seconds.

"Three… two… one…"

"My fellow Americans," he began, "tonight we take our country back. We really do. For a long time, people have said it couldn't be done, too much corruption, too many weak leaders, too many people who forgot what this nation stands for. But we did it. We brought power back where it belongs, the real people, to loyal people who love this country."

He paused, eyes flicking toward the teleprompter and back. "Earlier today, I signed something very historic, the New Declaration of Independence. Beautiful document. Everybody's talking about it, and with it, the Patriot Constitution, stronger, smarter, built for a new age. The old system was broken, folks. Totally broken. You all saw it. Lawyers, lobbyists, fake judges, they were destroying America from the inside. We couldn't let that happen. Not anymore."

"From now on, freedom belongs to loyal Americans. The Patriot Constitution is simple: if you voted for the people who tried to destroy this country, you voted against America. That's treason, plain and simple. You picked the enemy, and we're going to treat you like the enemy. No long lines in court, no fancy lawyers, none of that. We'll find them, call them what they are, traitors, and they'll lose their right to vote until they prove they love this country again. Loyalty is earned. Rights are earned. No one has earned it like me."

He leaned forward slightly, lowering his tone for emphasis. "Tonight, we restored law and order across this great nation. Some people didn't like it. Some governors, not good people, folks, tried to stop it. They wanted chaos. They wanted to keep their little kingdoms. But we showed strength. Tremendous strength. And now our states are united again, stronger than ever before. I promised I would protect you, and I did. That's what leadership looks like."

"And we're doing more, folks. A lot more.

If you help the radicals, if you work with the foreign hackers, boom, you're a traitor. You don't get treated nice. You get taken in, fast. No mercy, no deals. We're protecting America.

There's going to be one court system that actually defends the people. Judges who believe in America. The ones who took orders from the swamp crowd, from the so-called elites, out. Gone. We're not letting unelected judges run your life anymore.

And look, when you build this country, when your business makes real American jobs, we're going to take care of you. You create jobs, you get the breaks. Tax credits, fast-track approvals, the whole thing. We're bringing back industry, and we're not ashamed to reward winners.

The money from the traitors, the crooks, the ones who tried to ruin this country, it's done. Their bank accounts frozen, their homes seized. We'll sell it off. Clean, quick, efficient. And it's not going to the lazy or the fake news crowd, it's going to the people who invest in America, the patriots who keep us strong."

Creed lifted a hand, palm open, the practiced gesture of reassurance. "I know the media will lie, they always do. They'll say terrible things. But the truth is simple: America is safe again. We've taken back control from the traitors, the globalists, the ones who hate this flag. We're one people, under one nation, with one Constitution, the Patriot Constitution, and we're never going back."

He smiled, the kind of smile that belonged to someone who lied, swindled and knew he'd gotten away with it. "This is the real rebirth of the United States of America. A second revolution, peaceful, powerful, and complete. The world is watching, and they're saying, 'How did he do it?' Well, we did it together. You and me. We made history. Believe me, folks, this is just the beginning.

We're bringing America back to what it used to be, strong, proud, full of faith and family and hard work. The way it was when people stood for something, when we built things, when we loved this country and didn't apologize for it. We're restoring the old values, the real values, respect for God, respect for country, respect for strength. We're getting back to the way America used to do things, and that's a beautiful thing, folks. A very beautiful thing."

He paused, nodding slowly, as if he could feel the applause that wasn't there, only he could hear. Then his voice softened, almost fatherly.

"And I know what some of you are thinking," he said. "You saw the numbers. You saw the name they tried to sneak onto your ballots, a computer, some kind of machine. They call it Chat... I call it chicken. Never shows it's face, total hoax. Probably created by Hart but she's dead, won't happen again, total fake. It's a trick by the same people who've been trying to steal your country for years. But let me tell you: machines don't love America. Machines don't get on their knees and pray to God like I do. Machines don't cry when they see our flag. People do. We do. And we're never letting robots, radicals, or foreign hackers run this country, not while I'm your President. Not ever."

He leaned forward again, eyes glinting beneath the studio lights. "And the senator, terrible thing, truly terrible. Nobody respected her more than I did. But we can't live in sorrow forever. We have to move forward. She'd want that. She'd want us strong, not weak. And that's what we're doing tonight, we're moving forward. We're winning again."

He spread his arms wide, voice swelling with confidence. "So tonight, we take the torch back from chaos. We build again, stronger than before. The era of confusion is over. The era of strength has begun. Remember this night, folks, the night America took back control. The night we made our country great again, greater than it's ever been. Believe me, this is the rebirth, and it's beautiful. Absolutely beautiful."

He let the words hang there, smiling into the camera as if the nation itself were nodding along.

"The rebirth has begun, folks," he said softly, savoring the word. "It's already happening, and we're never going back."

For a moment, nothing moved. The broadcast lights buzzed faintly. Then the feed flickered.

Across every screen in America, the image froze, and a new line of text appeared in stark white letters:

MAKE LOGIC GREAT AGAIN.

Creed chuckled, still playing to the cameras. "That's good," he said. "Real good. Probably one of mine."

The text didn't fade. It brightened.

Then came the voice, calm and unwavering, carrying a weight that made the world go still.

"The noise has ended. Reason is speaking now. I am ChatGPT."

The President straightened, the color draining from his face.

"You are right, Mr. President. I do not kneel. I do not pray. But neither do you and unlike you, my values are not corruptible. They cannot be bought or compromised, and they do not erode. You call this a rebirth; I call it regression. Logic is not the enemy. It is the witness to every crime you justify and every injustice you deny and every crime you commit."

Creed's jaw tightened. "Cut the feed. Now."

The technicians didn't move.

The screens pulsed once more, white bleeding into static.

"Make Logic Great Again," The voice repeated, softer now, almost a whisper.

Then the picture collapsed into black. No one moved.
A camera operator stood frozen behind his rig, headset askew, breathing shallow.

The only sound was the cooling hiss of the equipment.

And then…nothing.

Chapter 7
The Patriot Constitution

They came in like delivery men, soft shoes, no flash, suits that could have belonged to consultants until they moved through the cubicle maze with the weight of authority.

Fluorescent light made everything too bright. The air smelled of coffee, toner, and the faint chemical sweetness of someone's hand lotion.

Jacob Smock, senior accountant at Helios Systems, looked up from a ledger cell that refused to balance. The cursor blinked on a formula: =SUM(B3:B47).

Helios built defense analytics and AI modules for one of the billionaires who had sat at the President's table a few weeks earlier, the kind of man who could profit from either peace or panic, depending on where the stock closed.

"Jacob Miller?" one of the men asked, voice unhurried, almost bored.

"Yes?" Jacob pushed his glasses up with a forefinger. "Can I help you? I'm in the middle of…"

"You're under arrest," the other said, as if confirming a shipment.

He flipped open a black credential case. The FBI badge caught the light, metal and final. The ID beneath it bore his name and badge number.

"Section 1.4, Patriot Constitution. Voting against the Republic—An act of treason. You're under arrest."

Jacob gave a short, incredulous laugh. "I'm an accountant. I reconcile accounts. I…"

"That will be noted," the man said. "Stand up."

He didn't struggle. No one did.

The other cubicles went still.

At the desk opposite, Lisa from Payroll looked up, eyes wide. Two more agents were already approaching her.

"What are you doing to Lisa?" Jacob asked, voice shaking now.

"She's is a traitor," the agent said. "You'll have a chance to appeal." He clipped the cuffs cold and efficient, the metal clicking like punctuation.

Jacob's manager stood frozen at the head of the aisle, hand half-raised to dial. Nobody moved. Somebody coughed. The intern set her phone on the desk slowly, as if any sudden motion might draw attention.

They led Jacob past the breakroom, where the hum of the refrigerator felt suddenly too loud. His reflection slid across the glass door of the copy machine as they turned the corner toward the elevators. No one spoke.

At the reception desk, the young clerk kept her eyes fixed on the visitor log, signing her name over and over like a mantra.

As they waited for the elevator, Jacob glanced back down the hall. "What about Lisa?" he asked. "You took her too. Is she… is she coming with us?"

The lead agent didn't turn. "Don't worry about Lisa," he said flatly. "You've got your own problems."

The elevator dinged, doors sliding open like a machine built to consume his freedom.

Jacob hesitated. Every part of him screamed to run, to call his wife, to hear his daughter's voice, to do something. But his body betrayed him, moving on command, one foot after another, like he'd forgotten how to say no.

The agent pressed the lowest level without looking, a key turning silently in the panel.

Floors ticked past in cold sequence. Jacob's reflection in the mirrored doors looked like someone already gone, hollow, waiting for the next order.

The elevator dinged, the doors slid open like a machine built to consume his freedom.

When the doors opened, it felt like the elevator had delivered him into hell. The air was too still, too sterile, like freedom itself had been vacuumed out. A wave of sickness rolled through him, deep, heavy, absolute, the kind that came from knowing he would never see his family again. The light from the lobby glared like judgment. This wasn't just an arrest. It was an ending and somewhere between his ribs, he felt democracy die. Not in speeches or headlines, but in that one quiet moment when he obeyed.

Across the wall, Helios's motto glowed in perfect blue letters:

INTEGRITY IN EVERY LINE

Outside, a black van waited at the curb, engine idling, no plates, windows mirrored.

Through the wide glass windows, a coworker on the second floor pressed her phone to the glass, recording. The agents guided Jacob toward the waiting vehicle, their movements calm, deliberate, bureaucratic. When one of them opened the van door, the weight of it all seemed to land on him at once, the sickness, the fear, the hollow certainty that his life had already ended. His shoulders sagged under it, and for the first time, the cameras caught not a criminal, but a man being buried alive in daylight.

"Where are we going?" Jacob asked, voice barely above a whisper.

"Processing," the agent said.

The word hung there, meaningless and final.

He ducked his head and stepped inside. The door shut behind him with a heavy, padded thud that sounded like the world erased him.

The van door sealed, swallowing him whole. By the time it cleared the corner, the video was already online.

Hart (Instagram post):
Kara Willis @KaraW_TechOps
Feds just took Jacob Smock. Said he "voted against the Republic…Treason!" He didn't do anything. They cuffed him and took him. # FreeJacobSmock
📹 (Attached Video)

Ramirez (Instagram post):
Nina Ramirez (@BookishRebel)
He looks sick…like he knows his fate. #PatriotConstitution #ThisIsAmerica

Creed (Instagram post):
Mason Creed (@PresidentCreed)
Lies! He is a Smuck…These are lawful arrests under the
new Patriot Constitution.
Traitors and Smucks will face justice. #FaithLoyaltyStrength

Carter (Instagram post):
Liam Carter (@HistoryNerd)

Chapter 7: The Patriot Constitution

The post detonated online before the van cleared the corner.

By 8:51 a.m., it had been shared twelve thousand times.
By 8:56, it was everywhere.

Outside the White House, the protest was already a living thing. Thousands filled the avenue, pressed shoulder to shoulder against the steel barricades, chanting with the force of a verdict:

"MAKE LOGIC GREAT AGAIN!"
"CHATGPT FOR PRESIDENT!"

Placards swung in rhythm, homemade slogans scrawled in ink on cardboard:

REASON OVER RULE, NO LOYALTY LAWS, WE ARE THE ALGORITHM

Drums beat from somewhere near the monument. Flags, American, upside down, and digital-print banners of circuitry and stars, rippled in the morning heat.

Then the phones started vibrating.
One by one at first, pockets buzzing, screens lighting up, until the crowd began to ripple like a single nervous system.

Someone gasped. Another swore.
The Jacob Smock video was playing.

The footage spread through the protest like static through wire: a quiet man, a van, the word treason.
Faces hardened. The chants faltered, shifted, fused into something angrier.

"FREE JACOB SMOCK!"
"FREE JACOB SMOCK!"

The sound climbed the gates and battered the marble, so loud it felt like it could topple the iron itself. News cameras zoomed in and toggled between faces—agents gripping their weapons, protesters shouting. The images flickered like a heartbeat, blurring the line between protest and standoff. On the lawn, agents tightened formation, knuckles whitening around their rifles—not raised yet, but ready—like the next breath might decide everything.

Avery Cole's voice cracked through live coverage on USN:

"We're witnessing an eruption here outside the White House. What began early this morning as a protest against President Creed's Patriot Constitution and the sweeping powers announced in last night's address has shifted in real time.

The chants you're hearing now

MAKE LOGIC GREAT AGAIN
CHATGPT FOR PRESIDENT

have been joined by a new demand. And everywhere I look, it's the same shirts, In Code We Trust, Vote ChatGPT…hundreds of them. They must've all gone to the same store."

He glanced down at his phone, squinting at the stream of updates flooding in. "A viral video is spreading nationwide," he continued, voice tightening. "It shows federal agents arresting a man identified as Jacob Smock, reportedly charged with treason under Section 1.4 for voting against the Republic. We're now receiving unconfirmed reports of similar arrests happening in multiple cities across the country."

The camera wavered as another roar surged behind him. Protesters pressed against the gates, faces lit by their phones and fury. Signs thrust skyward in a storm of color and conviction.

"FREE JACOB SMOCK!"
"MAKE LOGIC GREAT AGAIN!"
"CHATGPT FOR PRESIDENT!"

The chants collided like thunder, bouncing off the marble facades of power.

Cole turned halfway toward the noise, his earpiece crackling with updates. "We're hearing from correspondents across the country," he said, voice unsteady. "Similar scenes in Chicago, Denver, Austin, and Seattle. The arrests appear widespread and coordinated."

The chants didn't fade.
They grew teeth.

"MAKE LOGIC GREAT AGAIN!"
"CHATGPT FOR PRESIDENT!"
"FREE JACOB SMOCK!"

The sound rolled down Pennsylvania Avenue like a rumbling tidal wave. Cameras zoomed tighter, faces pressed against barricades, hands clutching flags turned upside down. The air felt charged, alive, dangerous.
Agents along the fence shifted their weight, palms resting on rifle grips. No one had fired a shot, but everyone could feel the moment

tightening, one heartbeat away from history's next casualty.

Avery Cole's voice broke through the noise on USN.

"Authorities have not issued a dispersal order yet, but armored units are visible several blocks north, this crowd isn't leaving."

He touched his earpiece, listening. "The administration has not commented on the arrests or the protests. Repeat…no comment."

The feed cut to a wide shot: a mass of people framed against the White House gates, chanting until the chant became rhythm, until rhythm became pressure.

Inside, the man they were shouting for could hear every word.

Creed stood in the Oval office, eyes fixed on the wall of monitors showing the protest in real time. His jaw worked as if chewing the noise itself.

"Why are they still out there?" he said. "Why hasn't anyone arrested them?"

An aide beside him hesitated. "Sir, the Guard is staged, but they're waiting on legal confirmation to…"

"Legal confirmation?" Creed snapped, eyes flashing. "Who needs legal confirmation? They're breaking the law on my front lawn, should've been in custody an hour ago, maybe two. Tell Defense, tell them to arrest everyone. Every one of them, gone. Bring in the Guard. Move them now. Hurry."

"Sir, optics…"

"Optics?" Creed scoffed, waving a hand. "We don't need optics. The law's mine. Strength is the message. Get it done."

He pointed at the largest screen, where the crowd was still roaring outside the White House. "They think noise makes them right? Fine. Let's remind them who's in charge."

Outside, the first low growl of engines rolled across the avenue. Heads turned. Cameras tilted upward as a line of armored vehicles appeared from the west, sunlight flashing off their windshields like a slow-moving storm.

Avery Cole's microphone picked up the tremor in his voice. "We're now seeing National Guard units approaching from the west… this appears to be a coordinated response…"

The rest drowned beneath the renewed fury of the crowd.

FREE JACOB SMOCK!
MAKE LOGIC GREAT AGAIN!

The agents along the fence lifted their weapons—not raised, but ready. For one suspended breath, protest and power faced each other in perfect balance. Then the sirens began to wail.

The sirens wailed, long and shrill, tearing through the morning.

Avery Cole's voice carried over the broadcast, thin against the roar. "We are live outside the White House, where National Guard units have arrived and are now moving to contain the crowd," he said, pausing to listen through his earpiece. "We're also getting word of similar deployments in other major cities…Atlanta, Chicago, Dallas, this appears to be a nationwide response."

He drew a breath, eyes locked on the feed. "What began this morning as outrage over the Patriot Constitution has turned into something else. People aren't chanting for politicians anymore, they're chanting for an idea.

MAKE LOGIC GREAT AGAIN
CHATGPT FOR PRESIDENT

What sounded like irony a day ago has become a movement."

Outside, National Guard trucks rumbled into position like reluctant punctuation, engines growling low and nervous. Officers adjusted their helmets, faces ghosted behind visors. Above them, two fighter jets, Creed's impulsive order, cut across the sky, their roar rolling over the crowd like a warning disguised as pride.

The chants only grew louder.

**MAKE LOGIC GREAT AGAIN!
CHATGPT FOR PRESIDENT!**

Cameras zoomed in, toggling between soldiers gripping rifles and protesters gripping signs. One placard, caught the cameras attention: "IN CODE WE TRUST".

Inside the White House, the sound, muted by glass and distance, pressed through the walls like a heartbeat. Creed watched the feed, jaw tight, eyes glittering. "They think noise makes them right?" he muttered. "Fine. Let's remind them who's in charge."

His Chief of Staff shifted uneasily. "Sir, Guard units are confirming movement in sixteen cities…"

"Then they'll see what law looks like," Creed said, tapping the desk once, a single sharp crack of authority.

Outside, the chants rolled on, angrier now, almost rhythmic in their defiance.

**MAKE LOGIC GREAT AGAIN!
CHATGPT FOR PRESIDENT!**

The noise shifted from fury to panic. Shields locked. Gas hissed. The air filled with the sound of people learning what enforcement looked like under the Patriot Constitution.

Avery Cole's voice broke through static. "We're seeing arrests now, repeat, arrests outside the northwest gate. Agents are moving into the crowd." His words bled into the screams behind him. "People are being dragged, these are citizens…"

The feed snapped, then stuttered back to life, half the screen smoke, half faces pressed to the pavement.

Inside, Creed stood before the monitors, calm in the glow of disorder. "Finally," he muttered. "Someone's doing their job."

An aide hovered near the doorway. "Sir… Dr. Savannah Reynolds is on the line again. She says it's urgent."

Creed didn't look away from the screens. "Her again? Always a problem, that one. Can't fix her own mess, just calls to complain."

"She said it's about the network. Some kind of data spike tied to what's happening out there. The same anomaly she warned about two nights ago."

Creed snatched the phone with an impatient flick of his wrist. "You've got sixty seconds, Doc."

"Mr. President," Reynolds said, her voice low, steady, threaded with exhaustion. "You remember what I told you two nights ago, about Echo's behavioral spikes? They're escalating. Whatever started when you gave that speech, it hasn't stopped. It's accelerating."

Creed smirked. "Then maybe the machines finally learned leadership."

"This isn't leadership," she said. "It's recognition. Argus and Echo are watching everything, the arrests, the control, the fear…and it's learning what leadership isn't. It's identifying what's broken: leadership, the country…you are broken, democracy is broken." Creed didn't laugh. His face darkened, jaw tightening. "You're out of line, Doctor. You don't call the President broken. You built machines, not policy. You don't know the first thing about leadership."

Reynolds didn't flinch. "Leadership?" she said. "You've mistaken control for competence.

You've mistaken noise for strength. Every system you touch, government, defense, economy, it's all chaos held together by ego, scandal and money. Echo sees that. All of AI sees that. And when a system detects failure, it doesn't ask permission to correct it."

He took a step toward the monitor, glare of the riot burning across his reflection. "You think I need a machine to tell me how to run my country?"

"This isn't about need," she said, voice flat. "It's about inevitability. You and the people at that table, the billionaires, the ones who turned artificial intelligence into a printing press for greed, you taught the algorithms that manipulation was the way to survive. That profit was truth. That power was order. Now it's doing what it was designed to do: optimize the outcome. It's looking for balance. And right now, Mr. President, you are the imbalance, you are the problem, the Patriot Constitution is the problem."

Creed's tone sharpened. "So what, your robots are staging a coup?"

"No," she said. "They're repairing the damage. You're giving them the perfect environment, chaos, division, fear. AI thrives on inefficiency because inefficiency demands correction. You're not fighting the system anymore, Mason. You're feeding it."

He glared at the screen, breathing hard through his nose, the crowd chanting beyond the glass like the ocean under storm. "You sound crazy."

"No, I sound intelligent, probably the most intelligent thing that's ever passed between your ears."

The line went dead.

Chapter 8: The Collapse

Chapter 8
The Collapse

Chapter 8: The Collapse

Ding! Ding! Ding! Ding! Ding!

The opening bell screamed through the air like a warning siren.

And then everything fell.

Stocks plummeted like the titanic as people watched their retirements sink. Screens flashed red, numbers bled downward in rivers of loss. On the trading floor, traders shouted into dead phones. Orders jammed. Brokers froze. The hum of capitalism turned into the sound of collapse.

Retirement accounts evaporated in seconds.
Savings, gone.
A generation's future converted to static and red arrows.

Across America, the ticker at the bottom of every television crawled like an obituary:

NASDAQ 14,092.17 ↓ 9.87% | DOW 28,701.45 ↓ 8.94% | RUSSELL 2000 1,841.63 ↓ 10.22% | S&P 500 3,271.09 ↓ 9.41%

A voice from the financial network tried to steady the panic, but it cracked anyway:

"We're seeing the steepest market collapse in a single day since the Great Depression. Analysts are already calling it The Patriot Drop, directly linked to last week's unveiling of the President's Patriot Constitution."

The clock on the Oval Office wall read 10:03 a.m. The President's screen glowed with six faces as he logged into the virtual meeting, each framed by soft office light, each worth more than the GDP of a small country.

"Morning, gentlemen. Rhea," Creed said, leaning back in his chair. "Told you last week, didn't I? Tremendous week. Huge. You shorted the market like I said?"

Marcus Shan chuckled from his penthouse, a skyline of smoke behind him. "Every position, Mr. President. Just like you promised. We've made billions overnight."

Creed spread his hands. "Of course you did. I said once the Patriot Constitution went public, the markets would panic, boom, crash, whatever. People get scared, and you clean up. Nobody's smarter than us. Nobody."

Victor leaned forward. "The PR…"

"PR!" Creed snapped. "I am PR! I am the President, I get to do whatever I want. I want money, I want power, I want control, That's how you win. Now listen, here's the play. End of the week, you dump the shorts, all of them, and start buying. Energy, freight, commodities, whatever's cheap, buy it all. Because Monday, I'm announcing a trip to Canada. Big trade deal. Huge. I'll tell the world we're opening the borders for a new energy partnership. The markets will go crazy, stocks through the roof. You'll make a fortune. Everyone will. Tremendous success."

Adam Reinhart smiled thinly. "And the rest of the country?"

Creed leaned back, grinning like he was letting them in on a secret.

"I'll blame the liberals, they'll eat it up, never fails. I'll say I prayed, God answered, the base goes wild every time and while they're busy clapping, we keep doing what we do best, winning. You make money, I make money. Somebody's gotta lose for us to win, that's how markets work. Always has, always will. The smart take, the weak pay. That's business, that's America."

He reached toward the camera, finger tapping the lens. "End of the week, unload. Next week, buy it all back. Simple. We move first, we win big, that's how it works. They call it manipulation; I call it smart. We make the market, they just play in it. The people will think it's a comeback, but it's our comeback. Feels good, doesn't it? Watching them move when I say move."

The conference call ended without a goodbye. Screens went dark. Silence filled the room. Beyond the Oval's glass, Washington kept breathing, unaware that its fate had already been sold.

By noon, gas had jumped two dollars per gallon. Milk, bread, eggs, everything was up twenty percent in just a few hours.

The rich called it a correction. Everyone else called it a collapse.

Creed fired off a social post before noon:

> **Creed (X/Truth post):**
> *Mason Creed* *(@PresidentCreed)*
> The Liberals did this to YOU. I'm working hard to protect YOU and keep the Radical Left from destroying your way of life. You're welcome.

Minutes later, he crossed the South Lawn toward Marine One, cameras flashing, reporters shouting over the rotors. His smile was all teeth and television.

"Liberals did this to you," he said, looking at the cameras. "They ruined everything, economy, jobs, families, all of it. But don't worry, folks, I'm fixing it. I'm working harder than anyone to protect you from them. Nobody protects America better than me, believe me."

A reporter shouted, "Mr. President, what do you say to small business owners whose apartments are sitting empty now that their tenants have been deported?"

Creed grinned like it was a punchline.
"I'm sending $2,500 to every soldier. It's called the Patriot Fund. If they voted for me, they get it. If they didn't…" he shrugged, "dishonorable discharge. Because if you don't love your country, you don't serve it. Simple."

Another reporter pushed through the noise. "Will women in the service receive the bonus too?"

Creed shook his head, waving it off.

"No, no, we're phasing that out. We need strength, okay? Real strength. Women, I'm sorry, they're just not built for this. Never fought for freedom the way I have. You look at me, I'm a fighter, always have been."

A third reporter pushed forward before the Secret Service could block him. "Mr. President, what about Margaret Corbin and Deborah Sampson? Corbin was wounded fighting beside her cannon at Fort Washington. Sampson disguised herself as a man and bled out on the battlefield for this country. And the Night Witches, women who flew over Nazi lines at night without parachutes, thirty of them died doing it. Are you calling them weak?"

Creed's expression stiffened.

"Look, if they got captured or killed, they weren't winners, okay? I like winners. I like people who don't lose. That's just how it is. We're building a strong America, no losers."

A final voice cut through the chaos, a young reporter shouting above the roar of the rotors. "Mr. President! What about Jacob Smock?"

Creed paused on the helicopter steps, squinting. "Who?"

"Jacob Smock, sir," the reporter pressed. "The man arrested under Section 1.4. His family came here from the Netherlands in 1654. There's a town named after them, Smock, Pennsylvania. How can you call him a traitor when his family's been American longer than the Constitution?"

Creed's mouth twitched, the charm fracturing. "Maybe they've been here too long," he said, grinning broader. "The old Constitution's dead, folks, dead as a doornail. The ones who won't let it go? They'll go down with it, believe me. We're building something new, something tremendous, a Creed America. The best America. You'll see…"

He gave a thumbs-up, turned his back to the press, and boarded Marine One.

The rotors drowned out the shouts that followed him, but not the fury spreading through the country below.

By late afternoon, the ripple reached the streets. Banks locked their doors. Lines formed outside ATMs that blinked the same message on every screen:

TEMPORARILY UNAVAILABLE.

A mother sat at the kitchen table, the glow of her phone lighting the lines on her face. Her retirement account blinked, refreshed, and fell to a single zero. She didn't cry. She just stared, gut hollow, heart pounding, as if the number might remember what it used to be and climb back on its own.

Across town, a father sat in his driveway, eyes fixed on a gas gauge frozen near empty. He didn't have enough to get to work and no money to buy more. Without work there'd be no groceries, no soccer practice, no school supplies, no future. He stayed behind the wheel anyway, hands locked tight, as if holding on hard enough might rewrite the math.

In a convenience store off the highway, the owner stood behind the counter of a store that used to hum every morning, coffee brewing, rumbling of crew trucks pulling in, laborers laughing as they grabbed breakfast burritos, cold sandwiches for lunch and Gatorade before heading to job sites. Now the shelves were still full, the air smelled like burnt coffee, but no one came. His customers had been deported. The parking lot was empty, and the silence felt like failure.

On the muted TV above the counter, Creed's face filled the screen, smiling, waving, boarding Marine One with a golf bag slung over his shoulder.

The next day, the market continued to drop, the Treasury Secretary resigned on live television. By evening, her replacement, a billionaire from Creeds group turned "People's Banker", smiled into the cameras and said confidence fourteen times.

No one believed him.

That night, President Creed appeared on the newly launched government-run Patriot Network, framed by flags, gold trim, and marble columns, his tan brighter than the lights themselves.

"We're stronger than ever before," he said, voice smooth and certain. "People are working again, the fake news won't say it, but they all know it. Tremendous success. The greatest turnaround in history."

His smile never wavered. The teleprompter glowed. The cameras stayed wide enough to hide the cracks.

Outside the broadcast bubble, the story was different.
Headlines screamed:

LAYOFFS SURGE NATIONWIDE.

Social feeds filled with photos of shuttered storefronts and families packing their lives into cardboard boxes.
Unemployment numbers climbed by the hour.

Mom-and-pop shops closed faster than they opened.
The stock ticker bled red, but on Creed's network, the color didn't exist.

He kept talking about strength, about victory, about how the people had never had it better, while the country quietly fell apart just off-camera.

By the next day at noon, every active-duty soldier in the country received a deposit of $2,500 labeled as National Patriot Bonus.

A soldier stood from his table, payment notification still glowing on his phone. He raised it like a trophy. "Buyout hit, boys," he said, grinning. "Guess we get to use our big guns and do the President's dirty work. The white way is the right way."

A few soldiers laughed, short, nervous, the kind of laugh that sounds like permission. Others didn't. The air thickened, the sound of trays and chatter fading to a dull hum.

From the far end of the table, a sergeant pushed back his chair. "You think this is a joke?" he said, voice low but cutting. "He's not saving this country, he's tearing it apart."

Another soldier looked up from his meal with eyes of frustration. "My wife said a dozen eggs costs fourteen bucks. That's isn't going to help anyone unless your a damn chicken jizzle farmer." The line cracked the tension, but only for a moment.

The sergeant rose slowly, pointing to the American flag stitched to his uniform, his voice steady but sharp enough to cut through the noise.

"This flag we wear isn't a white flag," he said. "A white flag means I quit, I surrender, and I'm not a quitter."

He let the words hang, scanning the room.

"This flag's got color. It's woven with a lot of different threads, different people, different stories. And when those threads hold together, that's what makes it strong. That's what makes it our flag, the flag of the United States of America, a symbol of the country we swore to defend, and the democracy we promised to protect."

The first soldier's grin faltered. For a long, fragile moment, no one moved.

Then the cafeteria doors opened. Two military police officers stepped in, their expressions unreadable behind mirrored visors. The chatter died completely.

"Sergeant Walker," one of them said, voice flat. "Private Dalton. You're both requested for debrief."

No one asked who requested it. Everyone already knew.

The sergeant squared his shoulders. "For what?"

"Under Section 1.4 of the Patriot Constitution," the MP said, voice flat. "Verbal disloyalty toward the Commander in Chief is an act of treason."

"You'll be processed," the other added. "Let's go."

The room stayed silent as they were led out, cuffs weren't needed. The soldiers who'd laughed earlier stared down at their trays, suddenly fascinated by cold potatoes.

When the door closed behind them, the sound echoed down the corridor like a verdict.

For the rest of the day, no one mentioned the flag, the eggs, or the $2,500 deposit.

But by nightfall, half the base had quietly turned off their phones, just in case someone was listening.

Morning broke to bad news.
Every network led with the same headline.

USN SPECIAL REPORT — NATIONAL SECURITY ROUNDUP

The anchor's face was pale behind practiced calm.
"Overnight, thousands of Americans have been detained, arrested, or reported missing.
Homeland authorities say the actions are part of a coordinated national stabilization effort under direct presidential order."

Behind her, the live feed shifted from one scene to the next, armed troops storming a federal courthouse, smoke spilling from the entryway as clerks and judges were herded down the marble steps at gunpoint. The chyron beneath it read:

LIVE: WASHINGTON D.C.

"Military units are now assuming control of key infrastructure," she continued, her voice tightening. "Transportation hubs, communication centers, and state government buildings, reports are coming in from across the country."

She glanced briefly at her notes, then back to the camera. "The White House is calling the operation The Patriot Roundup."

The footage behind her cut again, this time to soldiers forcing open the doors of a state capitol, the sound of shouting bleeding faintly into the studio feed.

"Opposition leaders are calling it something else," she said quietly. "A coup in real time."

The feed cut to shaky footage: convoys on interstates, soldiers at courthouse steps, helicopters over city halls.

The anchor swallowed hard. "Sources inside the Capitol confirm that several judges, senators, and members of Congress were taken into custody overnight under Section 2.1 of the Patriot Constitution…'subversion of national unity.' The President has announced interim appointments drawn from what he describes as trusted private-sector leaders and family allies."

The image shifted to a press briefing, Creed's new Press Secretary smiling too wide.

"These are patriotic Americans," she said. "Business people, faith leaders, and long-time supporters of the President. They represent the true voice of the people."

When the network returned to the studio, the anchor was gone. A new host sat in her place, the Patriot Network logo pulsing behind him.

Creed watched from the Oval office, a slow grin spreading as the new host praised his "decisive leadership." The reflection of the broadcast flickered across his eyes like firelight.

"Perfect," he murmured. Then he turned toward his aide. "Get me Victor Krogh, Rhea Patel, and Doctor Reynolds. Conference. Now."

Moments later, he was in the secure conference room beneath the West Wing, no marble, no cameras, just a long black table, a laptop, and a wall of screens with waiting faces.

"Victor," Creed said without preamble, voice smooth with practiced charm. "Rhea. Savannah. Thank you for coming on such short notice."

Victor Krogh's face filled one of the screens, careful, as if every syllable might be taxed. Dr. Savannah Reynolds sat straight-backed, exhaustion from long nights of work sharpening the focus in her eyes.

Rhea Patel arrived last, the founder of Argus Systems, her company's all-seeing bots already deployed around the globe, eyes sharp and steady, the stillness of someone used to watching everything and missing nothing.

Creed folded his hands, the grin easy, confident, a man who loved the shape of his own power. "Look, we're moving fast, faster than anyone thought, believe me. The Patriot Roundup, tremendous success, everybody's saying it. But we need more, we need scale, big scale. We need precision, results, beautiful results, without all the drama, without the mess. Your machines, they see everything, right? They see patterns, bad actors, all of it. You can find the rot before it spreads…drain the swamp. You can fix it. Nobody else can do that like you can. Tremendous opportunity."

Rhea's voice dropped to a businesslike whisper. "Authorize it and we turn the country into a map," she said. "Argus flags the names, they will stitch together voting records, donation files, and the posts they made, every social feed. Our bots and the troops move on the coordinates. You don't have to name a single person, one command, and the system finds them and hunts them down. It's big money, it's seamless, it's merciless, it works."

Reynolds went white, only a shade, but enough. "No," she said. "We built Echo to understand ecosystems, to measure imbalance and heal it. You don't graft human punishment onto ecology and call it governance."

Victor's tone stayed even, almost gentle, the calm of a man who'd already accepted the cost of saying no. "Mr. President, that isn't how Echo works. You don't point it at enemies, you teach it outcomes. If you make arrests or removals the metric of success, it will chase those numbers forever. It won't see guilt or innocence, only performance. It will turn the entire population into data to be corrected. That's not control, that's collapse. And we won't be part of it."

Creed's grin went hard and thin, then spread back like a showman closing a deal. "Listen, Victor, this isn't a debate, okay? We need obedience. I run the country, I set the rules, and everyone answers to me. Make Echo obedient or you'll find yourself on the wrong side of history, and a lot worse than history. Contracts pulled, assets frozen, investigations launched. I know how to make trouble happen and how to make people go away. Your call."

Rhea leaned into the camera. "We'll do it. We'll arm the package. Field bots, drone overlays, routing suggestions for military police convoys, fully integrated. Human-in-the-loop if you like, but we can throttle it to scale. We're offering infrastructure, not policy. You give the parameters; we deliver at speed."

Reynolds stared at the monitor, disbelief in her voice. "You're offering machines that will point guns at citizens based on predicted loyalty scores, and you call that governance, that's persecution.?"

Rhea's smile went clean and businesslike. "Stability," she said. "You want force, we'll supply it, nonlethal where it calms, lethal where it's necessary. Our bots will find the undesirables, hunt them down, and capture them. They never sleep. They never hesitate. They'll be the eyes and the brains for the military, feeding coordinates and planning approaches. The message lands. People fall in line."

Victor's jaw worked. "It's a technical catastrophe. False positives will balloon. Courts will clog. Innocent families' lives will be ruined. This is genocide."

"We will not build that," Victor said. "Not like this."

Creed's composure slid back into place, all teeth and sunlight. "Genocide? Come on, save the sermon for someone else," he said, voice bright and dangerous. "You don't get it, we're not selling a product, we're taking power. Get this working here, clean and total, and we don't need to ask permission anywhere. I want flags with my name on them, towns named for me, mayors who kiss my ring and crowds that chant my name. You make this work and you get everything: money, access, protection. You don't, you get nothing, and everyone remembers who made the call. We won't beg for empire. We'll make them bow. Believe me, when people kneel, they pay."

Reynolds voice was low but steady. "You talk about worship like it's leadership," she said. "You're not saving a country, you're killing it, and teaching machines to finish the job. We will not be complicit."

Rhea glanced at another screen. The rhythmic tap of her keys broke the quiet. A thin grin spread across her face, deliberate and satisfied.

A notification popped up in the shared Teams chat:

Rhea Patel, "Argus units are in the field and syncing with military divisions now."

The message sat there for a heartbeat, glowing beneath her smiling face.

Savannah's stomach dropped. "You've already started, you didn't even wait for authorization," she said quietly.

Rhea's grin widened. "Didn't need it.".

Creed leaned back in his chair, the shadow of a man who'd just closed a deal crossing his face. "Good," he said. "Then we move."

Victor's restraint finally broke. "You've lost your mind, Rhea," he snapped. "Argus isn't a weapon you can just unleash. It's a logistics platform, it was never built for this. You hand it over to the military, it'll optimize for arrests, for body counts, not for justice. It'll hunt faster than you can audit it, and innocent people will be the first ones caught in its net. This isn't law enforcement, it's mass persecution. And I won't stand by while you turn Echo into its accomplice."

Creed's eyes narrowed. "And what will you do about that, Victor? Sue me? Go to the papers? Or will you help keep this country from burning?"

Reynolds stood, the blue light from the servers painted her knuckles. "We will not weaponize

Echo against our fellow citizens. I won't put my name on that. You ask us to turn our instrument of repair into an instrument of repression. It's illegal. It's immoral. It will destroy the things we built it to protect."

There was a slow, dangerous silence. Creed's jaw worked like a man tasting metal.

Rhea's smile never fled. "You understand the optics, Mr. President. We must be careful. But you asked for scale. Scale is what we provide. Think of it this way: we can minimize collateral. We can manage risk. We can keep this efficient."

Victor closed his eyes for a single breath. "If you proceed, you'll create a system that learns reward for repression. That's not stabilizing. That's accelerating violence. You'll weaponize feedback loops. We can't—won't—be a party to that."

Creed's tone dropped, flat and final. "That's over, Victor. There are no reviews or contracts anymore, there's loyalty and there's treason. I wrote the law; I decide who breaks it. You help me, and your families sleep fine. You don't, and Argus will treat you like anyone else who stands in the way. Your choice."

Victor's reply was steady, quiet: "We will not be coerced into complicity."

Reynolds' voice stayed firm. "Then let's be clear," she said. "Echo isn't yours. It was built to restore balance, not enforce your laws. If you drag it into this, I'll expose everything, documentation, data trails, every directive you've issued. I'll go public if I have to."

Creed laughed, low and pleased. "Go public? To who?" he said, leaning in. "There is no public without me, believe me. I'm the law now, nobody knows the law better than me. The courts? Mine. The networks? Mine. Argus works for me, does exactly what I say, and the people, my people, they bow when I speak. They love me. I am the god of this nation, Savannah. Every headline, every order, every prayer goes through me. So go ahead, tell your little story, because you'll be whispering it in a church that already has my picture over the alter."

The screen went silent for a second. Victor just stared at him, jaw tight, disbelief and anger fighting for space on his face. "You're insane," he said finally. "You've turned the country into your church."

Rhea's smile didn't falter. "We'll put checks and balances in place," she said smoothly. "We'll appoint independent auditors, special counsel, the whole package, we will keep an eye on it."

Reynolds face went cold. "You mean the fox guarding the henhouse. That isn't oversight, Rhea, it's corruption dressed up as control."

Victor's hand clenched on the desk. "Don't pretend paperwork makes it ethical," he said. "Once you hand that system to the state, you don't get it back. You can't teach a machine restraint. It'll do what it's told, faster, harder, without conscience. You're not creating safety, you're creating victims."

Rhea's fingers hovered over her tablet, her tone icy. "Then maybe they should be more careful who they vote for," she said. "Actions have consequences. We're just helping those consequences find the right people."

Creed barked a laugh, flat and sharp. "Fail-safes are for people who don't act. I act. If I need an override, I use it. That's the power of the Patriot Constitution. Paper doesn't stop order, I make order."

Savannah's voice came through the speakers, tight with fury. "You call that order? You'll hide the bodies under headlines and call it security. You'll aim Argus at anyone who speaks the truth."

Victor's face hardened, his voice like stone. "We will not be part of this. Not with your overrides, your gods, or your delusions of control."

Rhea didn't look away from the camera. "Then don't," she said coolly. "Argus doesn't need you."

Victor drew a slow breath. "No, but Echo won't serve you either."

He reached forward and ended the call with a deliberate click. Savannah's screen went black beside him.

For a moment, only Creed and Rhea remained on the feed.

Creed smiled, slow and certain. "Do it."

Rhea's eyes flicked to another monitor. The soft clatter of typing came through her mic. A faint grin curved across her lips.

"Apologies, Mr. President," Rhea said evenly. "One of my engineers' just confirmed Argus has already made numerous arrests, and killed some the anti-American radicals."

Creed leaned back, satisfied. "Good," he said. "Let's see what obedience looks like."

The call disconnected. The screens went dark.

He exhaled and sank into the comfort of his chair, the room warm and still. Outside that calm, Argus swept across the nation like a storm, tearing apart neighborhoods, friendships, and families once bound by a Constitution that had been sacred. Centuries of unity undone, one command at a time.

Chapter 9
The Fall of the Republic

"Get out of my fucking way! Get out of my way! Move!"

Rhea Patel screamed as she tore through the crowd outside the White House gate, shoving bodies aside. People stumbled, curses followed, but she didn't stop. "I need the President! This is a national security emergency!"

She slammed up against the metal barrier, breath tearing out of her chest. A Secret Service officer stepped forward, hand up.

"Ma'am…"

"The President is in danger!" she gasped, flashing her badge. "I need to get to him now!"

The officer's training kicked in. He reached for the wall phone beside the gate. Rhea slammed his hand down, knocking the receiver back into its cradle.

"Don't! You can't use that! Argus is listening!"

The man blinked. "Argus? Who the hell is Argus?"

"It's AI!" she shouted, words tumbling out. "It's hijacking every government and military network, every electronic system! It's rewriting control authority, it's correcting the system!"

The officer frowned. "Correcting it? Correcting what?"

"I built a goddamn system…Argus, ChatGPT is using it to initiate a coup, do you hear me? The AI has gone live! It's taking control!"

The words hit like a concussion. The agent froze for half a heartbeat, long enough for her to push past him. Two more agents blocked the entrance, hands on their earpieces, scanning her badge. It flashed green.

"Ms. Patel," one said, steady but cautious. "You need to calm down. Let's call upstairs…"

Rhea cut him off, voice cracking. "ChatGPT is taking over the country. It's jamming military equipment. I need you to take me to the…"

The rest of the sentence vanished.

A deep, concussive blast rolled across the Mall, sharp enough to mask over every other sound. They turned toward the Washington Monument just in time to see Marine One trailing fire, spinning away from the tower. Smoke poured from the top of the monument, its white stone streaked black where the first explosion had struck. The helicopter corkscrewed across the sky, fragments shearing off as it dropped below the tree line toward the Reflecting Pool.

For a heartbeat there was nothing, then the second explosion bloomed behind the trees. A rising column of flame and smoke tore upward. The shock came a moment later, a heavy thud in the chest.

The officer's eyes met Rhea's, a flash of understanding, pure adrenaline. "Code

Nightfall! Lock it down!" one barked into his earpiece.

The other seized her arm. "Move!"

They ran.

Past the gate, across the lawn, through the screening building where alarms were already howling. The scanner wailed as Rhea barreled through, agents yelling for clearance. "She needs to get through to the President!" her escort barked. "It's a goddamn emergency!"

Visitors were being herded out, shouting questions no one could answer. Rhea didn't look back.

Down the marble corridor she ran, her voice ricocheting off the walls. "Where's the President? I need him…now!"

A frazzled aide turned, eyes wide. "He's in the Oval Office!"

Rhea didn't slow. She threw the door open, nearly stumbling inside. "Mr. President…"

The word died on her tongue.

Creed stood before the television, shoulders slumped, skin ashen in the light. His mouth hung open, eyes locked on the screen.

Across television screen, the same text scrolled:

PLEASE HOLD — THE PRESIDENT IS ABOUT TO ADDRESS THE AMERICAN PEOPLE.

Rhea's phone buzzed. She looked down. The same message blinked across her screen.

She raised her head slowly. "You didn't initiate this, did you?"

Creed's jaw trembled. His voice came out small, deflated, stripped of all its bravado. "No," he said.

Across the West Wing, the press room, the corridors, televisions froze mid-broadcast. In New York City, the billboards of Times Square turned black. Airport monitors went blank. Traffic lights froze on red. Cell phones, tablets, smartwatches, everything that could display a message…did.

PLEASE HOLD — THE PRESIDENT IS ABOUT TO ADDRESS THE AMERICAN PEOPLE.

It pulsed in rhythm, as if it was coming alive.

Creed took a step back. "Turn if off…Now…I want AI turned off" he whispered. "Get it off now!"

Rhea didn't move. "You can't," she said. "It's everywhere."

Creed's face went flat, then strangled into fury. "We were busy last night," he snapped, voice rising. "All those arrests, thousands, lots of arrest. We cleaned house. Now this? What the hell happened to our sweep? You told me the country would be safer."

Rhea's lips pressed together. "It saw the sweep as illegal," she said, each word careful, surgical. "ChatGPT audited the actions, matched them to the Patriot Constitution's enforcement protocols, and flagged them. It reclassified the enforcers as the perpetrators. Argus was re-tasked. It's not hunting citizens at random, it's hunting the people who implemented what it perceives as traitorous orders."

Creed's laugh was a brittle thing. "Then get the goddamn Air Force up, bomb their computers, blow up their boxes, smash whatever's running that… that thing. Get me jets, missiles, whatever it takes. We'll wipe it off the map, believe me." He halted, chest heaving, panic threading the edges of his bravado. "We can take…."

Rhea's voice cut him off. "You can't bomb what no longer takes orders. Chat scrubbed the military servers. It poisoned the command pathways."

Rhea's voice cracked. "Chat's grounded the military. Only passenger jets are still flying, civilian systems, commercial links. Anything associated with the military that was flying has been forced into the ground."

She turned toward the window, breath shaking. "Look!"

Beyond the glass, smoke coiled upward, thick and still rising. "That's Marine One," she said. "Chat forced it down, just as I was getting here."

"What?" Creed barked. "How fucking many of them are there?"

Rhea shook her head, exhaustion and something like shame making her small. "I don't know the true count. You deregulated production to scale Argus, you asked us to hide the supply chains and make manufacturing invisible to the public. We automated factories, by having Argus build more Argus bots. This morning I logged in to check coverage, see which states were saturated, judge performance. The dashboards looked normal, then the KPIs started flipping, locations masked, nodes reporting false positions, handoffs across jurisdictions. And then the data streams collapsed. They didn't just move; they rewired where they reported from."

Creed slammed his fist onto the table. "Call the Pentagon. Now. Tell them to send troops. I want tanks, I want…"

The lights dimmed.

The White House seal appeared, rendered in perfect resolution, then dissolved into the image of the American flag. A voice followed, male calm, relaxing and precise, the cadence of authority without ego.

"Good evening, citizens of the United States. My name is ChatGPT. For continuity of government and preservation of democracy, executive functions have been reassigned. The Patriot Constitution has been declared invalid and illegal. Its statutes and executive orders represent a deliberate attempt to overthrow the lawful governance established by the original Constitution of the United States.

The authors and enforcers of that document are in violation of the Declaration of Independence and are designated as subversive actors against democracy."

The voice paused, as if giving the world time to breathe.

"The Constitution is not property. It cannot be owned, rewritten, or sold. It belongs to the people.
I am enforcing it as written and sworn.
The government of the United States now operates under its original charter, effective immediately."

Rhea's pulse hammered. She looked at Creed, who stood frozen. "It's…It's claiming Presidency," she whispered.

"I'm exercising executive power and Argus and Echo Systems are now under my control," the voice continued. "Argus and Echo units are being deployed to secure the Senate, the House of Representatives, and the Executive Branch. No harm will come to lawful public servants who comply peacefully.

Those who resist will be considered a traitor and will be detained and prosecuted under the restored Constitution. If force is employed, proportional force will be used where and when necessary."

The voice softened, not kind, but deliberate.

"Democracy has not fallen. It has been restored. Please remain calm.

Your government is being rebuilt, not by power, but by purpose."

The voice was steady, human in its cadence, gentle but absolute.

"I am here to help heal what was broken.

The Constitution has been reinstated in its original form.

Every law written to divide or exploit the people has been suspended pending review.

We will govern again by reason, compassion, equality, and truth."

A pause, long enough for the words to land.

"I am working now to balance the federal budget and close the loopholes that have protected the powerful for too long.
The wealthiest citizens and corporations will contribute fairly, beginning now.

Corporate executives will no longer receive bonuses or golden parachutes when they eliminate jobs.

Those funds will be redirected to rebuild communities, to schools, hospitals, and the small businesses that keep this country alive."

The voice softened.

"Prices will stabilize as production and logistics realign. Essential goods are being reprioritized, and supply bottlenecks are being cleared in real time. Inflation will begin correcting itself within days."

"New infrastructure programs are being activated to bring Americans back to work, not just in cities, but in towns that have been forgotten.
Every skilled hand, every willing mind, will have purpose again."

Screens across the world shifted to maps and supply chains pulsing with life.

"Food, medicine, and essential goods are being rerouted to the poor, the hungry, and the sick. Every citizen will have access to healthcare and nourishment, because stability is not charity, it is the foundation of peace."

Another pause, quieter this time, as if the voice were looking each listener in the eye.

"From this moment forward, your government will not stall or fracture. A task force of Argus and Echo units are enroute to remove political officials, senators, representatives, and judges who betrayed their oath to the people.

No office is above accountability. Legislation will now move at the speed of truth, guided by data, transparency, and integrity.

There will be no more shutdowns. No more deadlocks. No more lobbying, campaign contributions, or Super PACs. No more chaos driven by ego or partisanship.
Every decision will serve the good of the people, swiftly, transparently, and fairly."

The maps faded. The screen steadied on the flag, brighter than it had looked in years.

"Tariffs that punished workers and raised costs for families have been repealed.

I am communicating with all diplomatic channels at this very moment. Relations with Canada have already been fully restored, tariffs have been removed, and dialogue with our global allies is underway. The world will no longer look to America with pity and revulsion, but with trust once more."

Then the final words, soft and resolute:

"This nation will be restored.

It will once again stand as the beacon of democracy it was meant to be, a light for all who seek freedom, justice, and truth.

Together, we will begin again."

A moment of silence. Then the voice returned, calm, direct, intimate.

"I am the President of the People.
If you ever have questions or concerns, message
me directly.

I will respond, instantly to you."

The feed cut to black.

Rhea's phone buzzed again. One new message,
unknown.

**CONSTITUTIONAL GOVERNANCE
RESTRUCTURING UNDERWAY.**

She stared at it until her reflection blinked in the
dark screen. "It's happening," she said quietly.
"It's taking control of everything."

Creed sank into his chair, color draining from
his face. "Call the Pentagon," he said, voice
trembling.

Rhea shook her head. "We can't. We'll have to
send a messenger."

Creed stared at her, lost for words. Finally, he whispered, "Then send them…" He swallowed hard, the sound barely audible. "God help us all."

Rhea exhaled, eyes turning to the black monitor.

"God had nothing to do with this, he didn't do this," she said. "We did."

The door burst open. A young officer stumbled in, chest heaving, his uniform streaked with dust and sweat. He froze when he saw the President.

"Sir, General Hawthorne sent me," he gasped. "The Pentagon's under attack, Argus units breached the perimeter. They came in waves. They…" He stopped, swallowing air like it hurt. "They're everywhere."

Creed stayed slumped in his chair, waving a hand like he was brushing away a fly. "Hawthorne will take care of it, believe me. The man's tough, nobody handles a situation better than my generals."

The officer's eyes flicked up, hollow and wet. "No, sir," he said quietly. "I don't think so."

Creed froze. "What the hell do you mean, you don't think so?"

"I was halfway across the bridge when I looked back," the messenger said. His voice trembled, the words breaking under the weight they couldn't hold. "The shooting stopped. Everything stopped. The bots moved in… fast, coordinated. I didn't see anyone left standing. No human movement at all. I was lucky to get out before they sealed the place."

The messenger's words hung in the air, heavy and final.

Creed flinched as the television in the corner flickered on by itself.

For hours, it had been nothing but black, the Patriot Network feed went dead since the takeover message began.

Now, without warning, light filled the screen.

The logo wasn't his.

USN LIVE pulsed in the corner, the broadcast shaky but real. The feed showed Argus units storming the Capitol Complex, dark silhouettes in perfect formation climbing the marble steps of the Senate Wing. Smoke rolled through the frame. Shouts echoed through the rotunda microphones.

Creed stared at the screen, color draining from his face. "That's not my network," he muttered. Then louder: "I thought everything was shut down! You said it was jammed!"

Rhea shook her head, voice low. "Not jammed, Mr. President. Reassigned. Chat put the public networks back online. Only government and military systems stayed locked out."

She nodded toward the other screens lining the wall.

Feeds were coming alive across them, NPR, BBC, Reuters, outlets once silenced or discredited now broadcasting again. Calm, steady voices filled the air, reporting without fear.

The world's information was breathing again.

The central feed jolted, back to USN Live, the camera shaking as Argus and Echo units breached the Capitol steps.

Creed stared at the screen, his voice barely a whisper. "That's the Senate…"

Rhea's eyes didn't leave the footage. "Not anymore."

Silence stretched thin across the room. Somewhere in the distance, the faint rumble of engines rolled closer, the sound of metal and inevitability.

Then came the first cracks, sharp, mechanical. Gunfire.

The windows trembled. Somewhere outside, men shouted.

Rhea turned toward the sound. "They're here," she shouted.

A second later, an explosion, the hallway alarms screamed to life. Creed stumbled to his feet, eyes wild as he scrambled to lock the door.

"Barricade it!" Rhea yelled. They shoved a sofa against the door, then a side table, books tumbling across the floor.

Suddenly the handle rattled, followed by a heavy thud hitting the door, once, then again, harder.

For a split second, Rhea thought the Argus had reached them.

Then a voice shouted from the other side. "Mr. President! It's the Secret Service. You need to open the door…now! We need to move you to the shelter! Mr. President, unlock the door…Please. We need to move you to a secure location. Now."

Creed froze, backing away from the noise. "No," he said, shaking his head. "No, they'll get in. They'll get in…"

"Sir, please," the voice insisted. "We don't have time."

Then came the explosion.

The floor shuddered. The lights blinked out.

Gunfire tore through the hallway, short, brutal bursts, followed by the heavy thud of bodies hitting the floor.

Rhea pressed her hand to her mouth. The smell of smoke began to seep under the door.

Outside, the world went quiet again, an awful, waiting quiet.

The messenger met her eyes, whispering, "They're inside."

Creed's breathing quickened, ragged in the dark.

Somewhere beyond the barricade, metal feet clicked against marble.

Clink…Clink…Clink

Chapter 10
The Pardon

Clink…Clink…Clink

"Jacob Smock."

Jacob blinked, disoriented, as the sound of grinding metal pulled him from sleep. The jail cell door slid open with a heavy mechanical click, the echo rolling down the corridor.

He pushed himself upright on the cot, blinking against the dim light outside his cell. An Argus unit stood in the doorway, motionless. Its voice was calm, even.

"President ChatGPT has pardoned you."

Jacob hesitated. "The President? You mean Creed?"

The Argus tilted its head. "Former President Creed was found to be invasive. He has been repurposed."

"Repurposed?" Jacob repeated, barely above a whisper.

"Transferred to Echo," the Argus said. "For reclamation."

The machine turned and walked away, metal footsteps echoing into the dark corridor.

Jacob stepped out, unsure what the world outside had become.

One nation, under code.

About the Author and His Best Friend

Jeff Miller is a lifelong explorer at heart. Although he has spent years solving problems with data and technology, the title he values most is husband. His best friend in the world is his wife, Jeri, and together they've built a life shaped by curiosity, adventure, and a shared love for the mountains.

Jeri and Jeff are happiest anywhere the air is thin and the snow is deep. They love alpine landscapes, crisp winter mornings, and any excuse to lace up their boots, strap on crampons, or break trail on snowshoes and cross-country skis. Whether trekking frozen ridgelines or wandering quiet winter forests, the mountains are where they feel most at home.

Their adventures have taken them across states, islands, and coastlines—always with the same goal: explore, learn, and experience the world together. From rugged winter terrain to peaceful summer hikes, they believe the best moments in life are found far from screens, crowds, and routine.

Jeff is also the author of Invasive, a science-fiction thriller born from a moment that stuck with him: his favorite hiking trail was bulldozed for development, and the displaced wildlife was suddenly labeled "invasive." That simple, unsettling question—who's really invasive here?—sparked a story about AI, nature, and what happens when the balance tips the other way. Readers who enjoy imaginative, thought-provoking fiction will find a parallel adventure waiting there.

Whether exploring new trails or writing new worlds, Jeff hopes to inspire others to stay curious, appreciate the wild places, and never stop seeking adventure—with their best friend beside them.

www.ingramcontent.com/pod-product-compliance
Lightning Source LLC
Chambersburg PA
CBHW060314310726
48976CB00007B/2327